W9-DBC-567

Last Train from Perdition

The Sequel to

I Travel by Night

ROBERT McCAMMON

SUBTERRANEAN PRESS • 2016

First Edition

ISBN
978-1-59606-738-7

Subterranean Press
PO Box 190106
Burton, MI 48519

subterraneanpress.com

What Has Gone Before...

In the year 1886, in his lair of the Hotel Sanctuaire in New Orleans, the adventurer and gun-for-hire Trevor Lawson lets his services be known by a card that reads *All Matters Handled* and, below that, *I Travel By Night*.

On a night in July, he receives a visitor from Shreveport. The wealthy lumber merchant David Kingsley has brought Lawson a letter from a man he's never met, named Christian Melchoir. In that letter, Melchoir states *Your daughter is very beautiful, Mr. Kingsley. And worth money to you, I'm sure. To return her to you, I require gold pieces in the amount of six hundred and sixty-six dollars. She is being held in the town of Nocturne, which is reached from the hamlet of St. Benedicta. Inform only one man of this, and send him to me with the gold. His name is Trevor Lawson.*

Kingsley wants to know what connection Lawson has with the abduction of his youngest daughter Eva, but Lawson doesn't know any man named Melchoir...though he does believe Melchoir wants *him* and is using the girl as a device. Lawson agrees to take the job, and tells Kingsley he will do his best to "return your daughter in a whole state".

Outside the hotel, Lawson discovers that Kingsley is being followed by a spindly figure in a black top hat and duster... and the chase is on.

Trevor Lawson is not only an adventurer and a gun-for-hire, but is also a vampire. He has taken the hard path of resistance to the forces that compel him to drink human blood and he subsists for the most part on the blood of animals...but he realizes that the vampiric Dark Society considers him a danger and desires him to be either fully in their fold or destroyed, and thus they send spies to watch him and—in the case of Kingsley's daughter Eva—use an innocent to lure him into what he knows must be a trap.

After a furious chase, Lawson confronts his quarry on the rooftops of the *Vieux Carre* and is stunned when the spindly vampire demonstrates an ability to shapechange into something more spiderlike than human. Lawson kills the creature with a silver bullet to the head, but not before taking damage himself. One benefit Lawson has discovered to his condition is that the injuries of broken bones and damaged internals will quickly heal. The only way he understands to destroy a vampire is with a silver bullet, consecrated with holy water, and delivered to the skull; thus a blood-hungry creature of the night breaks apart and burns, and is scattered in ashes by the unforgiving winds.

As dawn is about to break, Lawson visits his friend Father John Deale, who supplies him with both the animal blood and the silver bullets and is his compatriot in Lawson's battle against the Dark Society. Lawson tells the priest his experience of the night before, and confides that he believes as vampires age they become faster and stronger and some adapt the shapechanging abilities. He tells Father Deale he knows he's walking into a trap, and that Eva Kingsley may have already been "turned", but he has to go. The priest listens intently, for he's had his own experience with the Dark Society: in 1838, before he took the priesthood, his hometown of Blancmortain was visited by vampires who claimed ten victims, including his wife Emily. Blancmortain is now abandoned and forgotten, but Father Deale knows the creature that used to be his wife is still out there, somewhere.

The town of Nocturne is on no map, but St. Benedicta is a logging town at the edge of the swamp and to there Lawson must travel by night on his horse Phoenix. On the journey, he reflects on the horror of how he was taken by vampires from the dying and wounded on the battlefield of Shiloh, where he fought as a captain for the Confederacy. He was fallen upon by a ragged hoard of them, all eager to bite throat, shoulders, chest...wherever their fangs could find purchase. They were upon him like ants on a piece of sugar candy, but before they could consume him they were thrown aside by a stronger and more dangerous presence... that of a beautiful black-haired female in red who calls herself LaRouge, and it is she who over a period of time drains Lawson of his lifeblood and "turns" him to the life of the restless and ever-thirsty undead.

In the darkness of a root cellar prison, Lawson had heard from a legless Confederate vampire the tale that if one could consume the ichor from the body of the creature who had turned you, there was a chance of recovery to the state of being fully human. Was it truth or a myth? There was no way of knowing. But emboldened by this, Lawson was able to escape his prison...and now his search is for LaRouge, to test the tale...truth or a myth?

In the meantime, his condition worsens and turns him away from the sunlight further into the world of night, yet he continues his profession as a way to keep his connection with human beings, and also as a way to find his path to the throat of LaRouge.

In a barroom in St. Benedicta, Lawson exposes a cheating gambler by the use of his "Eye", a psychic power that allows him to roam through the often-twisted hallways of the human mind, learning the secrets that are hidden there, and also to manipulate human thought. An attempt on his life is stopped by a bullet from the dark, yet no gunman steps forth to lay claim to a truly extraordinary shot.

St. Benedicta's dockmaster tells Lawson everything he knows about Nocturne: a town of mansions, opera house and concert hall built deep in the swamp to rival New Orleans, but destroyed by a vicious hurricane in the year 1870 and long abandoned. The builder of that town? A possibly deranged young man from a rich family. His name... Christian Melchoir.

Lawson sets out in a rowboat but dawn catches him. He has brought along a black canvas shroud he is able to sleep in during the day, provided he can find shade, and it is in this state of vampiric repose that he hears another rowboat coming.

The young woman who has followed him tells Lawson her name is Annie Remington, but Lawson quickly realizes she is Ann Kingsley, Eva's older sister. As Annie Remington, she travels with a show for the Remington Firearms Company performing trick shots, and it was her bullet that put an end to the attempt on his life the night before. She tells Lawson she couldn't allow him to be shot, for she's determined to follow him to Nocturne to make sure her sister is released and that Lawson himself is not behind the kidnapping.

Lawson wants no part of Ann accompanying him to Nocturne, but she's adamant and unrelenting in her desire to go with him. Lawson says he can't explain about his sleeping in the shroud just yet, but if she will wait until nightfall he'll tell her why and then she can make up her own mind about continuing on to Nocturne…but he would much rather she turn her boat around right now and head back to the relative safety of St. Benedicta.

At nightfall, Trevor Lawson emerges from his protective shroud and goes to great lengths to explain to Ann just who he is, what he is, and what he's fighting against. He tells Ann that Christian Melchoir, most likely on the command of LaRouge, has taken her sister to draw him to the Dark Society because they consider him a traitor and a threat and they wish to destroy him, so what he's rowing his boat toward is definitely a trap…one that will ensnare Ann as well, if she joins him.

Her reaction is summed in three words: "You are insane."

"All right," he answers. "*Row.*"

When they reach Nocturne, they hear merry music coming from one of the half-submerged and moss-laden mansions. Many boats are roped there. A party is in progress.

Lawson and Ann are invited up the rotten staircase into a ballroom where vampire musicians play and creatures of the Dark Society dance and whirl across the boards, their shadows thrown large by the candlelight upon the moldy green walls. At the center of this festivity is a chair with a woman wearing dirty clothes roped into it, a black hood over her head, the head slumped forward and the body slack.

Christian Melchoir introduces himself, and by this time Ann Kingsley realizes that what she has stepped in is not a custard pie.

As Ann goes to release her sister, the figure in the chair throws aside the loosely-tied ropes and stands up, and taking the hood off LaRouge reveals herself and asks Lawson, "I think you've been looking for me?"

Surrounded by the vampires eager to tear him apart, Lawson reveals his own secret…he has brought dynamite in a harness under his waistcoat. He lights the fuse and tells Ann to get out however she can. Then Lawson takes hold of LaRouge to test the myth, even as he knows he has less than a minute to live…but at least by draining her ichor, she will be totally and certainly dead.

Melchoir attacks, shapechanging to a winged figure, grasping hold of Lawson and tearing him away from LaRouge. He thrusts them both out a window into the night, as Ann fights for her life using silver bullets that Lawson has given her. Melchoir and Lawson crash into the steeple of a ruined church, and there Lawson is able to draw his derringer and put a silver bullet into the head of Nocturne's creator.

Lawson hangs onto the church steeple, his ribs broken and spine nearly snapped. In a weakened condition, he hears LaRouge calling for Christian Melchoir but ashes cannot answer.

Quiet falls. As dawn begins to break, Ann appears with a skiff below the church and Lawson pushes himself off the roof into the boat. Ann had fought her way out of the mansion, gotten down in the mud of the swamp and stayed there all night. She tells him that she watched some of the vampires row away in their boats, but some remain in the rotting mansions.

Lawson knows that many will be here, but LaRouge—whom he has heard called the queen of the Dark Society—will have already gone.

His quest must continue, but first he has some dynamite that could be very useful to blow this accursed town to pieces and with them the hideous sleepers in the shadows. He must be quick, because already the weak sun is making him burn.

Though shaken, Ann is still resolute to find her sister though Lawson has told her that Eva is likely already turned. Ann tells him she wants to join him in his fight, that she would be useful to someone who travels only by night, because she could walk freely in the daytime world and be his eyes by sunlight.

"Will you let me help you?" Ann asks, as Lawson prepares to blow Nocturne and its sleepers to Kingdom Come.

It is a heavy burden, to allow a human to help him. He knows the risks...but he realizes that to find LaRouge and end his torment, either by death or by returning to the human condition, cannot be done alone, and thus his answer is...

One.

"YES," HE HAD SAID NEARLY six months ago in the ghost of a Louisiana swamp town, after a night of almost unspeakable horror. He'd been answering a question posed to him by the woman who now stood at his side, and that question had been: *Will you let me help you?*

Trevor Lawson wondered if Ann ever thought of that affirmative reply as a curse, or as a sentence to be cast into the world of the Dark Society. There could be no return from that world without victory, and victory might be impossible but it was sure that flesh would be torn and blood would be consumed through hungry fangs.

He hoped, as he listened to the shrill voice of the wind that seemed to make this building shudder, it would not be his fangs that did such work on her throat. Or any other fangs, if he could help it.

If.

A dangerous word.

They had entered through the building's back door. They ascended side-by-side up a stairway to a door inset with frosted glass as gas lamps hissed upon the walls. Small diamonds of ice glittered on their hats and coats. A freezing rain had settled in just after nightfall. The weather prognosticator in the day's edition of the *Omaha Bee* had by chicken bones, Indian dreamsmoke or telegraph reports predicted the eastward movement of a tremendous storm swirling itself down from Canada, sure to be as the reporter wrote, a "veritable behemoth of a snow-thrower", indicating that he was paid by the word. It was early December of 1886. Any simpleton could see from the swollen bellies of the dark clouds hiding the sun all afternoon that the front edge of winter was going to be very sharp this year.

Trevor Lawson and Ann Kingsley had together come to many doors since that hot July night in Louisiana. Any door might open into the maw of the Dark Society, and Lawson knew they waited for him. They tracked him. They watched him from their holes, their basements, their ruins. They felt him in the currents of the night just as he felt them when they got close enough. He knew they must be so much better at this sense than he, but it was a condition growing stronger in him. Part of the "gift" they'd given him, one of many such. He could laugh himself to tears over that but now on those rare times when the heartsick pain lanced him deeply enough and he had the fluid to spare his tears ran red down a gaunt face that was becoming the color of the finest white paper sold to any scribe in New Orleans, his choice of home. Or rather to say, losing all color except that of the moon. He was writing his own story, month by week by day by hour. His story was one of great loss, of hardship, of time spent as a family man and young lawyer in Alabama, then on to the battlefield of the War Of Secession. He'd felt it was his honorable duty to serve, and instead he had been served.

Served up, to *her.*

The one in red. The creature who had turned him.

She watched him now, through many eyes. He was sure of it. Sure also that there were humans in service to their cause—their war against the daytime world—for whatever such befouled humans could gain from that dubious enrichment. Perhaps she watched him through human eyes, so he couldn't breathe her essence of perfumed evil and know how close she stood. If only he could see her, could find her...if only...

If.

A dangerous word.

Upon the frosted glass of the door was painted in bold black letters *R. Robertson Cavanaugh, Mining*

And Investments. There glimmered light beyond: what appeared to be a double-wicked candelabra whose two small yellow flames wavered back and forth like luminous cat's-eyes. "The correct place and the correct time," Lawson said to Ann, as he noted the hour of eight on his silver pocketwatch. He returned it to the pocket of his ebony waistcoat, sewn from Italian silk. Under his long black leather coat with a fleece collar he wore an expensive gray suit. On his head was a black felt Stetson with a cattleman's crease and a thin band made from rattlesnake skin. If he was turning inexorably into more of a horror than he already was, he figured he should dress well doing it. As an adventurer and sometime gun-for-hire he could thankfully afford such indulgences. And around his narrow waist—if not his *raison d'etre* then certainly his reasonable companion—was the black holster that held two backward-facing Colt .44s. The Colt on the right had a rosewood grip and the Colt on the left had a grip formed of yellowed bone. Each pistol held six slugs. The gun on the right side held regular lead bullets, while the one on the left did not. Lawson had been instructed to enter the office directly at eight. He reached for a brass doorknob polished by many wealthy hands. As he did he saw Ann wince just a fraction and he knew exactly what demon had surfaced from her mind.

Another door to be opened. Another threshold to cross, and what lay within?

She had dreaded doors and thresholds since Lawson had returned with her to her father's mansion just outside Shreveport after the events of July. Under a scythe of a moon they had found the barn's doors open and David Kingsley's prized horses gone. The nightblack house was empty, though its front door was also wide open. The servants were not to be found. Kingsley did not answer his elder daughter's calls. The flare of the oil lamp that Lawson had bought in the swamp town of St. Benedicta on the return trip revealed evidence of violence. Firstly, a painting of Ann's cherished mother, dead from consumption these last ten years, had been torn from the wall and ripped apart. *Shredded* would be the word.

And secondly, in the library where Ann's father in brighter days liked to take his repast by smoking his cigars and reading the classics, if horse-racing news might be called such...

Lawson had heard the hideous humming of the flies at work beyond the closed door before Ann had. Without horses to nip upon in barn or pasture, the flies had come in through a broken window and surely filled the room like roiling clouds. They worked by night as well as by day, and like the vampires they were voracious and greedy in their feasting.

"Enter," said a rough voice beyond the frosted glass of this new door before Lawson could turn the knob. Of course the man in there could see their shapes illuminated by the gas lamps. The personage who had summoned Trevor Lawson from New Orleans sat nearly in complete darkness save for the double candles. Lawson understood; the letter had said this was a very personal matter. Sometimes those were best left to the mercies of the dark.

He opened the door and went in first, with Ann right behind him. He had the feeling she wanted very much to draw her own Remington Army pistol from beneath her violet-colored coat, if just as a precaution, but she did not and he thought that was good: though their worlds of existence were both far apart and by necessity like joined shadows thrown by the same light, she trusted him.

"Two of you," said the man who sat behind a desk that seemed as broad as a Nebraska cornfield. "I expected only yourself, Mr. Lawson."

"My associate travels with me," was the response. "Pardon my not telling you that in the return letter."

"Is she good with a gun?"

"I am," Ann said, and the note in her voice told him he ought to believe it.

Lawson said, "I hope that gunplay will not be the first requirement for this job. I prefer it to be the last."

"As do I," answered R. Robertson Cavanaugh, "but where I will ask you to go, you'll need bullets, a steady aim and a cool head."

"Ah." Lawson offered a thin smile. "A destination I've already visited."

A silence stretched. Lawson might have thrown his Eye into the head of R. Robertson Cavanaugh to learn everything in a few seconds, but the silence itself spoke. The heaviness of it said that this was a man who was careful in his dealings with people, that he probably did not trust people very much nor necessarily *like* them, and that he had secrets he wished to keep close to his chest. He was a gambler also, for he had gambled that Trevor Lawson would come all this way by train from New Orleans simply from a letter that already had Lawson's business card in it.

It was a plain white card, this one a little smudged around the edges revealing that it was no youngster. Beneath Lawson's name and the address of the Hotel Sanctuaire was the line *All Matters Handled*. And below that: *I Travel By Night*.

The letter itself had been brief, written in blue ink by a strong hand: *A very personal matter. See me in Omaha, 8 p.m. 10th December. R. Robertson Cavanaugh Mining And Investments office, 1220 3rd Street. Discretion of course.*

Signed, *Cavanaugh*.

The gambler's hand had been aided by the inclusion of a banker's check for one thousand dollars and a series of railroad tickets for sleeping car service on connecting lines that would get Lawson to Omaha on the appointed day. Lawson had not failed to note that the tickets were all for night trains.

It had been a small matter to pay for Ann's tickets for her own berths in the sleeping cars, and then a slightly larger matter to gird himself for a long trip that might yet put him within reach of one of his most furious enemies, the sun.

"There's a key in the lock," Cavanaugh said. "Turn it."

Ann did. "Sit." It was spoken like a command. There was only one chair before the desk. "Another chair in the corner. Drag it over. I wasn't expecting a woman."

"And here you have a lady," Ann said. She lifted her chin slightly in a little display of fire. Lawson thought she'd earned the right, as she'd seen sights that would drive R. Robertson Cavanaugh gobbling mad and cause him to cast what appeared to be a barrel-chested bulk diving out the canvas-shaded window behind him. Lawson started for the extra chair, but Ann said, "I'll get it," and was already tending to the task.

He couldn't help but admire her. She had followed him from the swamp and been with him on several jobs for clients. Hers were the eyes that could bear the steely heat of the sun. They were as black as charcoal and fixed with an intense purpose that could frighten even a vampire. For the month of October she'd gone back to her name of Annie Remington and done a stretch of trick-shot shows for the Remington Company. But, alas, though her aim was ever true her heart was no longer in such displays, and as Lawson worried They could attack and take her at any time, and They would either tear her to pieces or turn her or use her in some hideous way best not dwelled upon, he was glad she'd moved into a room in the Sanctuaire on the floor just above his.

After all, she had no home to go back to. She would never go back to that house, where the flies made so merry.

Ann was twenty-four years old, she was tall and lithe and had light brown hair that fell about her shoulders. She was wearing a dark purple jockey's cap, a style she favored. Her chin was firm and square and her nose was sharp and tilted up at the tip. She was a very attractive woman, if one was attracted to a female who could blow a bullet hole through the eye of the King of Diamonds while it was on the fly. She was good and she knew it, and therefore of immense value to Trevor Lawson.

When the two visitors from New Orleans had removed their coats and settled in their chairs, R. Robertson Cavanaugh folded a pair of big-knuckled hands on the green blotter that sat like a small island upon a golden sea of wheat-toned wood. He wore a black suit and a black stringtie over a plain white shirt. His large head was bald, his ears prominent as if pushed forward to gather every whisper in the finest parlors and lowest dives of Omaha. He had a black beard shot through with gray, his eyebrows being all gray set as thickets above a pair of deep-set brown eyes that held no warmth nor charity, but rather only chill and caution. His nose and mouth were small for such a large face, adding to the impression of a human battering-ram.

He was not one to waste time on pleasantries or small talk. "Do you have any idea who I am?" The question was directed to Lawson.

"I would've made inquiries, but as you made a point of discretion I did not."

"That's good. Two years ago you helped the brother of a friend of mine. A preacher in Oklahoma kidnapped a fourteen-year-old girl from his congregation. He went raving-mad and thought she was the rebirth of the Virgin Mary. He was trying to get her to Mexico to start a new religion with her as his bride. My friend's brother is the one who paid you, he was—still is—the town's bank president. It was more self-promotion than civic duty, but it's seemed to solidify his position there. Do you recall?"

"I do." A complication had been that Preacher Shine in his own past life had been known as Handsome Harry Ravenwing, a killer of note who with a sawed-off shotgun had sent to their otherworldly rewards eight men, two women, a little boy and a federal marshal's horse in a robbery and murder spree from Arizona to Texas. Preacher Shine had still been carrying the shotgun when Lawson had caught up with he and the laudanum-dazed young girl in the cactus-stubbled nighttime badlands just on the Texas side of the border. The girl had been returned relatively unharmed to her father, while Preacher Shine alias Harry Ravenwing had flown away with a .44 bullet between his eyes. A mad dog on a holy mission could not be brought in tame on a leash. Lawson particularly was challenged on that job because of the large distances he had to ride on his horse Phoenix, under the threat of sunlight, but even two years ago he could dare at least the dawn and dusk more comfortably than at present.

"I got your card a roundabout way," Cavanaugh went on. "Needless to say, I didn't spill any beans to my friend except to say I needed the help of a professional."

Lawson was about to say *I am here,* but he corrected himself before it was spoken. "We are here. What's the nature of your problem?"

"I'm a rich man," said Cavanaugh. "A well-connected man."

"Undoubtedly."

"I have aspirations and a solid foundation of loyal customers and supporters. In fact I am in the process of conversations that might direct me to the United States Senate in the near future."

"Congratulations," said Ann with a bit of an edge to it. Cavanaugh paid her no attention. He kept his small dark eyes focused on the vampire sitting across the desk from him.

"You're very pallid, sir," came the remark that Lawson had expected. "Even in this light. May I ask...are you ill? Is that the reason you travel only by—"

"I have a skin condition that sunlight affects. My eyes also are afflicted. But you can be sure I—*we*—are able to get the job done."

"If history is truthful, then I have no reservations on that account."

History was indeed truthful, Lawson thought. No *ifs* there. He knew what he looked like: lean and raw-boned, pale as a New York accountant, a tracery of blue veins at his temples carrying the strange ichor of the vampiric tribe, clean-shaven because he no longer had to shave—a result of his condition—and blonde hair combed back from a high forehead and left shaggy at the neck. Likewise, he no longer needed the clippers of a barber's shop. His blue eyes were intense and clear, though sometimes he thought that a mirror could catch the spark of red embers in their pupils, though this image was fleeting and it might have been his imagination only. He had been called handsome by the wife he had left behind and by the female creature who in a blur of red had gone for his throat and afterward whispered with crusted lips at his ear, *I'm going to make you my finest creation.*

Trevor Lawson appeared to be a man of about thirty but that counting of years no longer mattered after April of 1862 at the battle of Shiloh. In human years he was fifty-four. In the counting of the vampiric span he was yet a child.

Though an angry child who sought not so much revenge as the freedom to live and die as a human being.

"I didn't want us to be disturbed tonight," Cavanaugh said. "I doubt there are many out because of the weather, but I take no chances that someone I know might see a light here and come up for a visit. As I say, I am well-connected."

"And secretive," said Lawson. "There must be a compelling reason."

Cavanaugh nodded. "My wife and I have three sons. One is a lawyer here, another works in the land trade business in San Francisco. It is my third son, the youngest, who is in need of your services just as much as I."

Neither Lawson nor Ann spoke; they waited for the rest of it.

"Eric was rebellious," the rich man of Omaha went on. "He hated the life of wealth and privilege. Why, when his brothers took to it so well?" The large shoulders shrugged. "Who can say? But he spurned every chance he was offered and went off to, as he told me, make his own life, on his own terms. We're speaking of a twenty-year-old here, who hardly knew his mind nor anything of the world. Well...he is twenty-three now. He has been educated by rough hands, and he wishes to come home."

"All right," Lawson ventured. "And the problem is...?"

"Eight months ago he threw in his lot with three other individuals. He understood they wanted to go north to work the goldfields of the Montana Territory. But on the circuitous way there, he realized they were cutthroats and thieves who thought they had discovered as wild a buck as themselves. They were recruiting new blood for their gang."

"New blood," said Lawson. He lifted his eyebrows. "Hm."

"He couldn't get away from them after he witnessed the first murder of a stagecoach driver. It's been difficult for him to get letters out, but he's managed to send two at the risk of his life."

"A high risk," Lawson said. "He's going by his real name?"

"No, he was smart enough not to use the family name. He's calling himself Eric James. He hasn't been required to kill anyone but he had to take part in two bank robberies in the Wyoming Territory, to prove himself. Thank God no one else was killed in those, or Eric killed…or captured by the law. Do you see where I'm headed?"

"A bad place," said Ann.

"Damn right," Cavanaugh answered, and for the first time looked at her as if she really had a role to play in this. His eyes slid back to Lawson's. "They have taken my son to their winter…shall we say politely…*quarters*. A town called Perdition, about thirty miles north of

Helena by rail. If those men find out who my son really is, they could hold him for an extreme sum of ransom. Plus…" He hesitated, staring at his clasped hands. "Plus," he went on, "my own future and that of my family would be destroyed."

Lawson had the picture, and it was not a pretty one. "You want us to bring your son home out of a snakepit."

"Eric wrote they have rewards on their heads from previous crimes. They're wanted dead or alive in both the Wyoming and Dakota territories."

"Their names?"

"The leader is named Deuce Mathias. The others are called Keene Presco and Johnny Rebinaux. They seem to be very good with their guns."

"What a coincidence," said Ann.

Lawson was silent. He listened to the wind shrilling outside the walls. The glass trembled in its windowframe. He was thirsty. His body ached. So did his soul. From a pocket inside his suit jacket he brought forth a small red bottle, a Japanese antique purchased in New Orleans. He uncorked it and wafted it back and forth under his nostrils. It was a heady scent that made iridescent colors bloom behind his eyes. Usually a spool of the thick crimson liquid would go into his favorite libation of rye whiskey, simple syrup and orange bitters, but tonight…

He drank just a sip, just enough to get a taste, just enough…

He recorked it and put it away.

"Good for what ails me," he told Cavanaugh. "My little sin."

"We all have them," was the rich man's response. He leaned forward on his blotter, planting his elbows like bulwarks to defend his pride, his ambition, and in this case also his desperation. In the eyes of that broad face perhaps there was a hint of pleading that this office had never witnessed by day. "Will you get my son out of there, and home?" Cavanaugh asked.

There was no need to confer with Ann. She trusted him as much he did her, and Lawson knew what she would've said, in his place. It was a job worth doing, especially for the extra two thousand dollars he would require.

He spoke for both himself and his associate.

His answer was, "Yes."

Two.

"READY?" LAWSON ASKED. "READY," ANN answered, with a purple-gloved hand's quick touch to the holstered pistol under her coat. They set off. Positioned some fifty yards from the front porch of the aptly-named Perdition Hotel was the completely misnamed—and misspelled, on its sign—Cristal Palace. Or it might have been wishful thinking, that a saloon and gaming house nailed haphazardly together with raw green boards and roofed with corrugated tin might somehow stand fast during a long hard Montana winter. For the moment it was standing, though half of it seemed to droop in sad acceptance of its ugly frontage. Its windows were glassless, covered with oilskin paper, its front door a curtain of canvas doubled to keep the cold from blasting through. Smoke rose through a chimney that might have been formed of metal cans joined one on top of another in a crooked insult to the builder's art, and was dashed away by the constant wind with an occasional flying pinwheel of indignant sparks.

As Trevor Lawson and Ann Kingsley crossed what was purportedly a street, Lawson contemplated how a heavy fall of snow could ease the most repellent features of a ramshackle town like Perdition. All yesterday and last night the white snow had come down. Inch after inch of it had first frozen and then shrouded the town's foundation of black mud. It had settled upon the roofs of the general store, the fledgling bank, the railroad depot and the assay office and made them groan like old men in tortured dreams. It had softened the hard vista of a primitive place situated in a valley between ancient mountains, from which the promise of a goldstrike was both a blessing to some and a curse to others depending on luck and fate.

Such was Perdition in gray twilight on the sixth evening since Lawson and Ann had met with R. Robertson Cavanaugh. They had been at the hotel since night before last. Not inconsiderable attention was paid to them, since their clothes and coats marked them as being on business other than the search for gold; indeed, it appeared that their strike had already been counted. But the people of Perdition were not ones to ask too many questions or nose into anyone else's business, as long as no claims were jumped and no killings were done in the street. At present the below-zero weather kept the miners in town, kept the Cristal Palace busy and raucous, and also in town—and sooner or later in that same Palace, Lawson guessed—would be the Deuce Mathias gang. He reasoned that wild bucks such as they would have a short resistance to cabin fever, and they would have to find steady release at either the gaming tables, the bar or the backroom bordello.

Lawson and Ann waited for a wagon carrying a load of barrels to creep past, leaving black trails in the snow, and then they continued on their route. Though the light was low Lawson wore his dark-tinted goggles. He was bundled up not from the cold, which had no effect on him, but from the needles-and-pins pain even this weak sun had on his exposed flesh. The sun was going down fast beyond the western mountains; it could not sink fast enough for the vampire gunslinger.

From the number of horses tied up at the hitching posts in front, the Cristal Palace was obviously doing a brisk business. As Lawson and Ann crunched through the snow they could hear the bad notes of a diseased piano being pounded and the shoutings and hollerings of rough men made happily stuporous by equally bad liquor. Last night the two searchers had been in the Palace for a couple of hours. There had been curious glances aplenty and one old miner had tried to dance with Ann, but after awhile they were treated as part of the scenery. They had been looking for any young man who fit the description of Eric Cavanaugh supplied by his father. The mission had not shown results. It was highly likely Eric would be sporting a beard and would no longer resemble as young a man as his father recalled, and likely also he would be in the company of at least one of the three gents who'd brought him here.

"We have to be cautious," Lawson had told Ann during the train trip from Helena in the late afternoon. Snow flew outside under dark gray clouds as the 4-4-0 steam locomotive pulled its coal tender, single red-painted passenger car and four freight cars through the mountain passes. There were six other passengers: a woman with two small children, a tall austere man who had the rigid bearing of a bible-thumper, and a man and woman travelling together who drank from a whiskey bottle most of the way, talked in slurred voices and gave out harsh laughter when nothing was funny.

"Cautious," Lawson repeated. He wore his dark goggles and was sitting in a corner where he could pull the curtains on the windows around him. The sunlight was nearly gone, and yet there was still pain. He wished he could wrap himself up in the black shroud he always carried in his bag but getting the attention that would bring was not wise. "If we find Eric here...a dangerous word, *if*...we're going to have to figure out some way to approach him without bringing the rest of the gang down on us. The only problem I have with gunplay is that Eric or some bystander might be hit. Not by us, by *them*." He noted the man he took to be a preacher staring at him from the other side of the car. The stare lingered for a few seconds and then the man looked away. *If* he only knew, Lawson thought.

Or maybe he does?

"We can't ask anyone about Eric," Lawson went on. "That would risk word getting back to Mathias and the others and we don't want them spooked. So the only recourse I think we have is to bide our time and visit the local saloons where such men might gather." He was silent for awhile and she was silent, and at last he asked, "Are you all right?"

"I am," she said.

But he knew she was not. How could she be? How could anyone be, who had seen what she'd witnessed?

In the Kingsley mansion in Louisiana that night, Lawson had not only heard the buzzing of the flies but had smelled the blood immediately upon entrance through the wide-open front door. It was human blood, aged maybe six days. Lawson figured it had been two or three nights after their episode with Christian Melchoir and LaRouge in the ghostly town of Nocturne. He reasoned she had led them on a raid here, and might have been joined by Ann's sister Eva if the girl had been turned.

"Wait here," Lawson had said, his eyes shining in the glow of the oil lamp he held. God help him but the rank aroma of the spill had quickened the flow of the black ichor through his own veins and made him nearly wild with hunger. It was all he could do to keep his head from snapping back and the rattlesnake-like fangs sliding forth to...what? Tear into the throat of Ann Kingsley?

"Draw your gun," he told her, his voice a harsh rasp. "Loaded with silver?"

"Yes." She had kept silver bullets in it since leaving Nocturne and during their journey through the swamp back to St. Benedicta. From there, they'd spent two days in search of a town from which the vampires might have gotten boats to reach Melchoir's bad dream. The nearest was a place called Sawblade, another logging town. Only it was deserted, not even a dog left in the soggy streets. A half-dozen boats had been pulled up on shore and hacked to pieces with axes, showing that some had escaped in the night before Lawson's dynamite went to work.

She had passed this way. Lawson was certain of it. As he and Ann had stood in the darkness with just the single lamp to light a path, and all the silent empty houses of Sawblade around them and even the crickets and frogs voiceless, Lawson had felt the passage of LaRouge here like a claw creeping across his cheek, scratching very lightly with razored nails at the back of his neck, promising *next time…next time…*

They wanted him—*she* wanted him—because he defied them. Because he clung to his fading humanity with his newfound vampiric strength, because he would not fall before the power of the Dark Society. He was a threat to them, a danger to their future on this earth.

He was an *if.*

If he fought them and won, would there be others who stood with him? *Could* there be?

Next time…next time. "Draw your gun," Lawson repeated.

"Do you think…one of them is in there?"

"I think one of them is out *here*. Draw your gun and if I lose control…just keep it ready." He needed a taste from his Japanese bottle of cattle blood to steady his nerves and dull his desires, but there was no time for that. The best thing to do was to get out of this house as quickly as possible, yet that closed door in front of him must be opened.

"Don't move," he told Ann. When he opened the door the rush of the blood-smell hit him in the face and set all senses aflame like a torch touched to pitch-soaked linen. It burned through him in an instant, nearly sending him to his knees. Or sending him at Ann

Kingsley like a ravaging juggernaut. He did not hesitate; he walked into the room and shone his lamp upon the scene of carnage.

She disobeyed him, but she had to. She stood a few feet behind him and to the side, and she had to turn away for a moment to be sick but Lawson needed her to look at the bodies. There were three, a man and two women. Not much left of them, but enough to tell what they'd looked like.

When Ann could speak she said, "Those...are the servants. My father is not here."

Lawson saw a declaration upon the pine-panelled wall. He lifted his lamp toward it. It was scrawled there in crusted gore, and as the flies spun around and around in angered clouds both he and Ann read the writing.

Revenge is a dish best eaten bloody.

"My father," Ann repeated, in a voice near breaking, "is not here."

They couldn't leave without searching the rest of the house. They did so with their pistols ready to fire a silver angel at anything that moved along the light's edge. But Ann was correct, as Lawson had figured she would be: her father was not there.

Once outside, Lawson had uncorked the Japanese bottle and had a drink of the cattle blood concoction that his friend Father John Deale procured for him from a New Orleans slaughterhouse. Ann had walked off a distance, even in the dark, and Lawson could say nothing to her so he let her alone.

She had as much to settle now with the Dark Society as did he. Lawson could image the vampires raiding her father's mansion, coming into the house like whirling blades on a violent wind, all fangs and claws and depraved desires. And he knew she must understand that if indeed her father and her sister were still alive and had been turned they would be yearning in their own fever to taste her blood and turn her.

It was their way, and they would not—could not—stop until all in this world travelled by night.

Piano music and harsh voices spilled out from the canvas folds of the Cristal Palace. Snowflakes whirled through the smoky air. Lawson and Ann stepped from the street's frozen mud onto the green boards of the sidewalk, and he started to push through the entry into Perdition's only den of entertainment.

But stopped.

He turned toward the direction they'd just come from, where the Perdition Hotel stood like an unsightly brown-boarded lump on the mound of a hill.

"What is it?" Ann asked, knowing he was sensing something beyond her reach.

"We're being watched from the hotel…second floor, third window from the right. A man was standing there. He just pulled back."

"One of them?"

"A human," Lawson said. He lifted his chin as if smelling the air like an animal. He sought what he'd come to think of as the "atmosphere of the unholy". Whether that was a particular burnt-flesh smell or a rushing of the ichor within him or simply the awakening of a sense of threat that humans possessed but was a thousand times stronger in the vampire he did not know. He just knew he had it, and it told him to be wary. "I'm not feeling any of them within close range."

"Someone just curious?"

"The man from the train was curious." Lawson had seen the man at the hotel when he and Ann were getting the keys to their rooms. Aboard the train, when the man had stared fixedly at Lawson once more, the vampire had thrown his Eye and entered the mind of Eli Easterly, for that was a name written in memory on the inside page of a well-used Bible, there in those corridors of the mind. Within seconds Lawson had walked through Easterly's mansion and found scenes there that told of a tormented life…a life still in torment.

"Well," said Lawson, quickly scanning the darkening sky, "we have work to do."

He pushed the canvas aside and they entered. The place was crowded, noisy and nearly stifling hot with all the bodies packed in and a pot-bellied stove burning wood at the back. Smoke from cigars, pipes and cigarettes swirled around the figures and floated in a blue cloud at the ceiling amidst a score of oil lamps hanging on nails. On the right side of the establishment was a long bar backed by a mirror in an ornate silver frame. A few tables were set around and in a corner out of the way was the music-offending piano and its player, a bald-headed black man with a long gray beard. On the left side of the Palace were card tables, a roulette wheel, a big spinner for Put & Take and various other stations designed to separate the crowd of miners from their money. In one sweeping glance the vampire gunslinger took in games of Faro, Keno, Mexican monte, Chuck-A-Luck, craps, Newmarket, and about as many variations of poker as there were tables. A winner's holler seemed to go up every five seconds, followed by an equally loud bout of cursing and otherwise bitter language from the losers. Eyes went to Lawson and Ann but didn't linger, because the wheel and spinner were turning, cards were being slapped down on green felt and ivory dice were tumbling.

Lawson made his way to the bar with Ann following close behind. He ordered a whiskey from a wizened bartender who likely kept a shotgun within reach at all times. "Anything to drink?" Lawson asked Ann, but she shook her head. Just as well, Lawson thought; the whiskey was something to toy with, for the strength of these potions was designed to further stupefy a man into betting against a dealer's high hand.

He reached back, unclasped the strap of his goggles and removed them. They went into a pocket of his overcoat, which he would be inclined to remove but that might bring the pickpockets stumbling toward him in an affectation of drunken friendship. As it was, here came the bar girls, two of them. They wore their makeup as if it had been applied by children just learning how to fingerpaint. Their frilly dresses were new, though, likely supplied by the management; one was as bright blue as Lawson figured the Mediterranean to be and the other as orange as an overripe pumpkin, which suited the woman's figure. On their way toward Lawson they took the opportunity to flick hats and press the backs of men at the tables. He saw others moving through the throng, all of them wearing the bright frilly dresses that must've come up by train all the way from San Francisco: pink as summer lemonade, green as a backwoods meadow, purple as a dream of passion, red as new-spilled blood.

Before Lawson had a chance to scan the crowd for the face of Eric Cavanaugh, Blue was upon him. She wore a frozen smile that must be painful to her jaws. The pain showed in eyes that were nearly as blue as the dress. She had blonde hair that had likely been pinned up earlier but now drooped from the weight of heat and smoke. Her makeup made her almost as pale as himself, her lips a garish slash of crimson and little spots of rouge coloring her cheeks. A small black beauty mark had been applied just at the corner of her left eye.

"Bu..bu...buy me a drink?" she asked, and if she had ever flinched at the sound of her own speech impediment those days were long gone; the way she held herself told Lawson she thought she was as good as anyone else here, or maybe she was just a very good actress.

"Certainly," he answered, and she asked the bartender for—of course—champagne. Which made Lawson want to smile at the preposterousness of it, but he thought his smile might frighten her off so he did not. This girl had not approached him last night; it had been a Chinese girl who seemed to know only how to say in English "Buy drink? Buy drink?" But he had a use for this one.

The walking pumpkin flashed silver teeth at Ann and also asked for a drink. Ann shook her head. The pumpkin immediately got a look from Hell's half-acre in her eyes. "You was in here last night," she said, as if in reproach. "What're you lookin' for?"

"Peace," Ann said.

"You a mite late," came the answer. "Church burned down last month." And with a flouncing of orange she turned away and strode with dignified grace into the midst of the gambling, hollering, cursing throng.

"What's your name?" Lawson asked the girl, who was probably seventeen under all that pancake.

"What do you please to call me?"

"Blue," he told her.

"Dandy. Then what do I ca...ca...call you? Whitey?"

"As *you* please. I'm also known as Trevor."

"You got a funny accent." Her eyes narrowed. "Not from around here?"

"From the south. I live in New Orleans." Their drinks came. Was it champagne or colored water? Didn't they know here that champagne should be fizzy? Lawson paid the bartender and touched his glass to Blue's. "To your happiness," he said.

She gave a quiet little laugh that had a twist in it, and when she sipped she watched him over the rim of the glass.

Lawson took the opportunity to let his gaze wander over the crowd of men. All he saw were hats, coats, and bearded faces, just like last night. He had Cavanaugh's description of Eric fixed firmly in mind, but this taxed even the powers of a vampire. Blue was standing a little too close to him. Her blood smelled spicy, like pepper and cinnamon. He wafted the glass of foul whiskey under his nostrils to mask her appealing scent; it helped only a little.

"Would you like to make some money?" he asked her, just before another whoop of triumph burst forth at the roulette wheel. No matter, Lawson thought; the winnings would be back in the pocket of the house within the next few spins.

"That's what I'm here for," she said, with a slight lift of her half-empty glass.

"All right." He dug into a pocket of his dark green waistcoat for a pair of silver dollars and put them before her on the bar. She glanced only casually at them, but he knew he had her. From here on, though, it was a dangerous ride. "We're looking for someone."

"Du...du..." She had to pause to get her tongue in working condition. "Do tell."

"A young man by the name of Eric James. I can't spot him in here because of all these beards. Do you know him?"

She gave Lawson a frown. "I figured you two might be the law. Openin' for a sheriff here, if you're interested. Last one got ta...tarred and feathered and rolled out of town in a ba...ba...barrel."

"We're not the law. We're private."

"Okey-dokey, if you sa...say so. What's this fella done?"

"Nothing. I just want to talk to him."

"Ha!" Blue smiled, though it was more of a sneer. "Come from New Orleans all this way to ta...*talk*? You ain't such a good liar."

"It's no lie. We want to talk to him. I'll tell you that he's in no danger from us, and in fact we're in a position to help him. If you know him, do you also know his friends?"

Blue didn't answer for a moment. She stared straight ahead and just over Lawson's shoulder, and he knew she was trying to decide in quick order many things: whether to trust a stranger, whether to betray someone that she likely spoke to or had relations with on a fairly regular basis, or whether to give a damn at all.

At last she said, "His friends are a rowdy bu…bunch. He's quieter than they are, kinda more refined."

The vampire gunslinger's gaze sharpened. He could easily send his Eye into her and draw out every secret, but it seemed a terrible violation. He would give her as much chance as he could. "Are any of them here?"

"They're all here," she answered without hesitation. She reached for the silver dollars, but Lawson's hand was so much quicker; he covered the coins long before she could get there.

"You haven't earned those yet." So saying, he drew a third silver dollar from his pocket and set it down amid the others. "I want you to do this: go to Eric's friends and touch them on the back, one after the other. Just make it casual, as you always would. Lastly, I want you to go to Eric and touch him. Tell him—as quietly as you can—to come to the bar. Speak the word 'Omaha.' Do you understand that? Afterward, come back here. You'll get your money and I'll buy you another glass of champagne."

She snorted. "Ain't real ch…ch…champagne."

"I'll buy you a glass of whatever you like, if you do what I ask."

Blue looked from Lawson to Ann and back again. Her gaze fell to the holsters under their coats. "Is there guh...guh..." She got it out only with an effort. "Gonna be trouble?"

"I don't know, but I will tell you again that we're trying to help Eric. Gunplay is not what we favor."

"Lots of gu...guns in here," she said. "Men been shot d...d..dead for even drawin' one."

"I'm sure. Our intent is to leave here without anyone being hurt."

Still she was not completely sold. "Eric's okay," she said. "His bunch...rougher'n six miles of ba...bad road. Wouldn't want to cross 'em."

"We'll take care of that." Lawson motioned toward the coins, which he figured was quite a payday for a girl in Blue's position. "They're yours, if you'll help us...and help Eric too."

"Help him to *what*?"

"Freedom," said Ann.

The way Ann had spoken that seemed to touch a chord in Blue. The saloon girl took a long look at Ann as if seeing her clearly for the first time. Then, abruptly, she shrugged her thin shoulders. "No sk...sk...skin off my ass," she said, and her eyes had gone distant. "I'll do it for two more dollars. Make it f...five." She tapped the bartop with her fist, which had diamond shapes tattooed on the knuckles.

"My pleasure." Lawson added the extra two silver dollars. "They'll be waiting for you."

Blue started to turn away and then stopped. "You ain't g…g…gettin' me in a damn m…mess, are you? I k… keep a clean nose."

"No mess. A valuable service, that's all."

She nodded. She stared for a moment at the five silver dollars as if they were her only friends in the world. Then she made a small noise of assent that might have been a word or might just have been a little breath of air escaping her lips, and she turned away to the task at hand.

Three.

"DO YOU TRUST HER?" ANN asked as they watched Blue move toward one of the Faro tables.

"We'll find out soon enough." Lawson took the opportunity to uncork his blood bottle and pour a little taste in to redden the bad whiskey, and he paid no mind that the bartender watched him as one might watch a dangerous and unpredictable animal.

Blue slipped through the crowd of men as the piano-player pounded the broken ivories and the cries of triumph and misery rang out. She stopped behind a man playing Faro and put a hand on his right shoulder, but he gave her no attention. Lawson and Ann saw that this man was slim and rawboned, had a mop of light brown hair and a slight darkening of beard. His brow seemed to overhang the rest of his long-jawed face and his eyebrows were dense brown thickets that met above the bridge of a hooked nose. He wore no hat but had on a red-plaid shirt and a gray jacket.

As Blue turned to continue her mission, an elderly man who appeared to be very drunk and too spritely for his own good came up and grabbed at her, but she smiled and dodged away with practiced grace. He stumbled into a poker table, upset the game and caused all manner of profanity to bloom. Then Blue was on her way again.

Lawson removed a thin Marsh-Wheeling cigar from inside his coat and lit it at the flame of a lamp on the bar. He drew the smoke in and exhaled it, aware that he might appear to be a man in need of sunlight but that he was far removed from the human breed. And growing further removed, it seemed to him, with the passage of every night. Even in this hothouse, he was always cold. True rest was something denied him, for in the daylight he slept as the vampires did: one part tranced, gathering strength for the hunt, and another part on edge, senses questing, fearful of discovery and the power of the sun to sear his flesh and burn his eyes out. Though he appeared strong and indeed was—also in the way of the vampire—his body was withering inside. He could not eat food, he could drink only a little, the taste of water sickened him, and the blood need was a constant pressure. The cattle blood was a poor substitute for what his transformation from human to monster desired, and though he fought it with all his power of will he did on occasion find a derelict in the darktime streets of New Orleans and take what he needed to survive a little longer.

It was LaRouge he needed to find. She, who had turned him. If he could find her, and drink her dry…

He recalled what he'd been told by another vampire, a legless Confederate named Nibbett, there in the root cellar where they'd kept him near the devastated battlefield of Shiloh. *After you feel and see and you* are, *you won't care to go back. Only way…is to drink the ichor from the one who's turned you. Drink it all down. Then you go back to what you were, and you* age. *Hell, some of 'em would turn to dust, if that was to happen. Ain't gonna be a thought in your head, though. All that goes away. You'll see. Trust an ol' rebel,* Cap'n. *Once you get turned…you ain't ever gonna want to go back.*

Lawson had escaped that house of hell by cutting off Nibbett's head with a butcher knife. He had been pursued by the horde, had jumped from a bridge into a river and that was the beginning of his story.

Where it might end he dared not think. If LaRouge and the Dark Society could not take him into the fold, bend and break him into becoming a true monster intent on consuming the life's blood of men, women, and children, they would have to destroy him. Tear him to shreds, scatter what was left of Trevor Lawson across the bloody fields of their war against humanity.

He was an *if,* and he could not be allowed to let others question their fates.

They were out there, watching him. They tracked him with powers and senses much older and keener than his own, he was sure. They waited for him to walk into a snare, and thus he was always so careful where he stepped. And yet…how else to reach LaRouge, but to let them get their claws on him?

He blew smoke toward the ceiling, his face grim and his eyes cold, and he watched the girl earning her five silver dollars.

She went to the group of men standing around the big Put & Take spinner. She touched on the right shoulder a tall, lean, black-haired man with streaks of gray at his temples. He was wearing a black suit and was clean-shaven, showing a chiselled profile that would have served him well among the ladies of New Orleans. He turned from the game, gave Blue a thin-lipped smile…and then his right hand came up and seized her chin with what appeared to be violent intent. The man was smoking a stub of a cigar, and he removed it to lean toward Blue and kiss her roughly on the mouth. When the man pulled back, the slick smile still on his face, Lawson saw Blue make a mistake.

Her eyes darted toward the bar and Lawson. They showed fear, and Lawson knew the man had seen.

But the man gave no reaction. He released her, said something to her, she nodded and walked away just as the saloon girl in the pink lemonade dress was moving in. A few heartbeats passed, and then the man slowly turned his head toward the bar, where his sharp-eyed gaze slid from one face to another until he came to the two he'd never seen before.

Lawson by this time was not looking directly at the man but could feel himself being examined. Now there was a sense of impending danger in the room; the man was not a vampire, but he had the second-sight of a born survivor. When Lawson next looked, the man was still standing at the spinner but he was tracking Blue as she pushed her way toward the roulette table. Lawson took a drink of blood and whiskey and said to Ann, "We've been discovered."

To her credit, Blue was still working for her money. At the roulette table she touched on the shoulder a heavy-set, brown-bearded gent who wore a black skullcap and a brown leather jacket with a fleece collar. This man, like the first, was intent on the game and gave no response. Lawson glanced quickly toward the gamblers at the spinner, and though the spinner was going around in a blur of red, white and black numbers the man who had seized Blue's chin was smoking his cigar and watching the girl as a cat might watch a mouse.

Blue approached another man at the roulette table. This man's back was to Lawson and Ann, but he had a mass of curly dark brown hair and he was wearing a navy-blue coat. She touched his shoulder, he looked up at her, showing a profile that included a full beard, and she leaned her head down and spoke.

Lawson could see her mouth form the last word.

Omaha.

"Get ready," Lawson said.

"For what?" Ann asked, but she was already as tense as an arrow about to fly from its bow.

He answered, "Anything and everything."

Eric Cavanaugh stared up at Blue for a few seconds as if he hadn't understood. The wheel was spun and he had not put down a bet. The little wooden ball clattered and clattered and clattered. The young man—older-looking than his father had described and made older and nearly unrecognizable by the beard—turned around to peer through the layers of smoke toward the bar. Blue was already on her way back to get her coins. Lawson's right forefinger went up to touch the brim of his Stetson, and both Eric and the gambler at the spinner saw.

There was a moment where the young Cavanaugh turned back to the roulette wheel and Lawson thought the rich man's son had no idea what was happening or what was about to happen. Lawson smoked his cheroot and waited, patience being one of his remaining virtues…

and suddenly Eric stood up from the table and began to wend a path to the bar.

At once, the clean-cut gambler at the big spinner—Deuce Mathias himself, Lawson guessed—tossed his cigar stub into a spitoon and started moving. Not toward Eric, but toward the heavy-set figure in the black skull-cap. Whatever was going on, Mathias didn't like it and he was alerting either Presco or Rebinaux.

Blue reached the bar first. She took the coins with a speed that would have been admired by any creature of a vampiric nature.

"You did well," said Lawson. "Thank you."

"Ain't exactly sure *what* I d…did."

Ann said, "Company's coming."

She didn't mean only Eric Cavanaugh. She meant that the oily-looking gambler Lawson had pegged as Deuce Mathias was approaching. Behind him the heavy-set man had paused to alert the younger one with the mop of brown hair at the Faro table. Mathias was wearing a gunbelt though the actual pistol was hidden by his black coat. The other two began their advance through the crowd as well, and they also were packing iron. None of them appeared to be appreciative of this sudden intrusion by strangers.

"Who are you?" Eric asked when he got close enough. He had sharp features and a look of wildness in his gray eyes. His face bore the weathered lines of hard living and perhaps the hard travels of many roads that led to regret.

"Your father's emissaries," Lawson said. "We're getting you out of here." Lawson's eyes went to the young man's gunbelt. "You do want to get home in one piece, don't you?"

"Home? My *father*?" Eric sounded genuinely stunned. "He...sent you?"

"Train leaves for Helena in forty minutes. We intend to be on it. Are you with us?"

"I...I...can't...they won't..."

"Eric?" The voice was as silky as the man's ruffled shirt. "Who are your friends?"

"My name is Trevor Lawson and this is Ann Kingsley." Lawson kept his voice light and easy. Ann had stepped to one side where she had a clear shot if need be. She was aware of the two others coming in from different directions. "Your name, sir?" Lawson prodded.

"I may be called the man who wishes you to leave this establishment," came the softspoken answer. His eyes were deep-set, icy blue pools that Lawson was sure had frozen many a victim. "You have no business here."

"Then we seem to be of different minds."

"Yours may be a bit *afflicted*. Easy, Johnny," he said to the young man who was showing a glimpse of a hogleg Navy revolver from underneath his gray jacket. "Let's give these two a chance to see another sunrise."

"Hm," said Lawson, with as much of a friendly smile as he could summon. He was well aware that his friendly smiles could frighten small children. "I don't really care for sunrises."

"I'm m...m...movin'," Blue said, and with the silver dollars in her fist she started to go past Mathias, but he reached out quick as a snake and grabbed her wrist. Her hand opened and there was the shine of the coins.

"I believe," said Mathias, "that there has been some *shit* going on here behind my back. Our backs." He twisted Blue's wrist enough to bring a wince of pain. "Nealsen, go about your business please," he told the bartender, who had paused in his pouring to take in the scene. Several other men at the bar were watching, and now they realized where the line of fire was and that they ought to be somewhere else. The black piano-player was still pounding the cracked ivories; he was unaware of the confrontation because his eyes were closed.

Mathias took the coins from Blue's hand and shoved her back toward Lawson and Ann. The girl's face showed red even under all the makeup. She shouted in a ragged and desperate voice, "That's m...*my* money! Give it back, damn you!"

Which brought an end to the piano-playing. With it the hollerings and cursings of the gamblers diminished as all realized a drama was being played out in their midst.

In another moment there was only the ticking of the big spinner going around and around and a hiss as an oil lamp's wick sparked overhead.

"Mr. Cantrell don't like no trouble!" the piano-player spoke up, indicating a soul who was either very brave or ready to be shot.

"Mr. Cantrell is not here right now," Mathias answered. His gaze never left Lawson's. "No trouble is intended. These strangers are on their way out."

Johnny Rebinaux had pulled his revolver. It hung in a loose grip at his right side. About ten feet to Rebinaux's left, Keene Presco had placed a hand on the buckle of his gunbelt but no weapon was showing yet. To emphasize the threat, Deuce Mathias pulled his coat back to reveal two Colts with black grips in their holsters. He pushed the five silvers into a pocket and then casually rested his hands on his hips.

"Now," he said, "before either you two walk out or are carried out…tell me the *why* of things. Eric, do you know them?"

"No."

"But they know you?"

"I…don't…"

"His father has sent us to bring the boy home," said the vampire. "Eric, he told us about the letters."

"Letters?" Mathias frowned, and now he was not nearly so handsome. He looked like a cunning predator on the hunt for fresh meat. “I am all at sea about this. What letters might those be?”

“He sent his—”

“I can speak for myself, Mr. Lawson.” Eric had found his courage, for the moment of decision had come. He was helped knowing gunfighters were standing behind him, even if one did happen to be a woman and the other looked to be as bloodless as a white stone. “I’m done with this life, Deuce. I want out of it. Yes, I wrote a couple of letters to my father asking for help, and I passed them to the post clerk. I want to go home. Can’t you understand that?”

“Eric wants to go *home*,” Mathias said to his compatriots, in a mocking tone. “Says he’s done with this *life*. Been sneaking around behind our backs, and us taking him in like family. Now that’s a fine plate of bad hash, isn’t it?” He turned his gaze again upon Trevor Lawson. “We’ll send the boy home, if that’s what he pleases. Seems to me his father must love his son very much, to send a couple of guns after him.” Mathias put one hand on the grip of a Colt. “Seems also,” he said, “that dear Father must have some money in his pockets. You two take back word to him…we’ll send his boy home, in due time.”

“Deuce, I’m leavin’,” Eric said. There was grit in his voice, but also a quaver. “I’m done with all this.”

“Leaving, he says.” Mathias was still speaking to the others. “After all we’ve been through together. No, I don’t think so.”

"Eric, walk out of here," said Lawson. His voice was quiet but commanding. "Blue, step aside."

"I want m..my m...*money*!" And with that she lunged at Deuce Mathias, going for the pocket in which the silvers resided.

What happened next was a blur to everyone but Lawson, and though Ann was fast she had not expected Johnny Rebinaux's speed and recklessness. His Navy revolver flashed up, catching yellow lamplight. Presco's gun was out, the hammer being cocked. Mathias was drawing both guns at once, and an instant before Rebinaux's pistol went off Mathias knocked Blue away from him with a wicked elbow. She staggered back as a haze of gunsmoke bloomed around her. Ann's pistol cracked and the gun in Rebinaux's hand blew to pieces, the bullet having hit the cylinder. He yowled with pain and danced a madman's jig, his gunhand torn open by jagged metal.

And then Presco and Mathias saw that Trevor Lawson was leaning against the bar, his Colt with its rosewood grip and load of deadly lead aimed somewhere between the two thugs as if he'd been standing that way for half-an-hour, yet neither one of them had seen him move from where he'd been half-a-heartbeat before. He was just *there*.

Their guns were still aimed at the floorboards, ready to shoot some sawdust.

Lawson blew a little O of smoke toward the ceiling.

"Drop them," he said.

Presco's pistol hit the floor. Mathias was thinking of gambling.

Ann said, "Damn! I was going for the third button on that little bastard's shirt!"

But Lawson knew she'd decided not to kill him, as death seemed such a constant these troubled days. Two more pistols fell.

The smell of fresh blood flooded Lawson's senses. It hit him like the need for whiskey would hit an alcoholic three days in the gutter. Rebinaux's hand was dripping red and he was sitting on the floor mewling like a hurt kitten, but the bloodsmell was stronger than that.

Then he knew.

"Oh…my God!" Ann said. She was already bending down to where Blue lay crumpled on her right side and the crimson was spreading around her.

The bartender started to reach for something under the bar. Without looking at him, Lawson said, "Don't do that," and Nealsen raised his hands and backed away.

"She's still breathing!" Ann started to turn her over and then thought better of it. "It's bad, she took it near the heart!"

"Clear this place," Lawson commanded. "Everyone out!" He didn't have to give that order twice. Money was scooped up, bottles were drained and cards were left scattered across the tables. The piano-player abandoned his instrument. Nealsen took a long drink from a bottle and he too took to the wind. "Stand with your backs against the bar and your hands behind your heads!" Lawson told Mathias and Presco. "Lock your fingers! Eric, is there a doctor here?"

"Yes, he's..."

"Go get him. *Fast.*"

Eric went, and then the vampire and the sharpshooter were left with the three dregs and the girl on the floor whose pooling blood began to make the ichor in Lawson's veins burn with desire.

Mathias showed a cruel smile. "Shall I give the girl her money now?"

Lawson came so close...so close to putting his gun's barrel against the man's throat and making him eat the last of the Marsh-Wheeling, but he was a gentleman and he would not stoop to such a thing.

"You've hurt one of my friends," Mathias went on. "Probably finished his gunhand, looks to me. Well...the girl got in the way, so I guess Johnny deserved it."

Johnny made a strangled sound, showing that he disagreed with the man's opinion.

"Take Eric and go on," said Mathias. "The girl's dying. Go on and take him to the train. If he wants to *leave* so badly. But I'll tell you this, sir..." And here the man's smooth voice became harsh and ugly. "I don't know what those letters said, but Eric James did some things the law would be very interested in. Now I can find out who those letters went to. Take me maybe five minutes with that post clerk. So take him on home, sir, and I'm glad to be rid of him."

"We could kill you all and be done with it," Lawson answered.

"Oh...you two may be hired guns but you're not natural-born killers. Otherwise we'd already be laid out on the floor."

"Jesus, Deuce!" Presco's voice was like a saw grinding over rusted iron. "Don't give 'em ideas!"

"Just giving him food for thought," was the reply, delivered with a nasty smirk. "Just food for thought."

Lawson was thinking about food. The feast of the vampire. The blood that was flowing from Blue's body only a few feet from where he stood. In fact, tendrils of the blood were reaching toward his boots, a further enticement to fall upon the dying girl and drink her dry. He shivered; he was so very cold.

In the distance the train's whistle blew, announcing an imminent departure. There were two trips a day, one in the late afternoon from Helena and one back in the early dark, the last train from Perdition.

Lawson could almost hear the girl bleeding.

Mathias laughed at some joke he had manufactured in his head. The wicks of the oil lamps overhead sizzled and hissed like a den of vipers, and beneath them the vampire gunfighter held onto his humanity with all the strength he could find.

Four.

THROUGH THE CANVAS ENTRANCE TO the Palace came not Eric and a doctor, but Nealsen and a broad-shouldered, beer-bellied man in a beaver-fur coat and black derby hat. He had a florid, pock-marked face and a brown beard that reached to the silver eagle on his belt-buckle.

"What the hell's goin' on in here?" the man shouted in a voice that nearly shook the timbers. He looked down at Blue and her life's-blood and made a face as if he'd bitten into a sour pickle. "Christ Almighty, what a mess! Somebody's gonna pay to scrub this damned floor!"

"Mr. Cantrell, I assume," said Lawson, his pistol still aimed between Mathias and Presco, as Rebinaux whined and clutched his mangled hand.

"And who the hell are *you?*" Cantrell almost thrust his face into Lawson's, but seemed to decide it was not a wise move. His eyes were bloodshot with rage as they slid from Lawson to Ann and back again.

"Bounty hunters from New Orleans," Lawson said, for he'd made up his mind what he had to do. "These three men are wanted dead or alive in the Dakota and the Wyoming territories. We're taking them to the federal marshall in Cheyenne."

"*Ha*!" said Mathias, with no trace of humor.

"You got papers?" Cantrell demanded.

Lawson produced his cowhide wallet with one hand and from it offered Cantrell a business card. Cantrell spent a few seconds studying the lines *All Matters Handled* and *I Travel By Night*.

He pushed the card away. "I don't think you two are proper bounty hunters. This thing don't smell right."

"Aromatics aside," said Lawson, "we're taking these men to Cheyenne. As your bartender probably told you, the girl was shot by *that* one." He nodded toward Johnny Rebinaux. "Helped in the endeavor by Mr. Mathias here. You see their guns on the floor. So...we regret the inconvenience to your profiteering, but we make no apologies for our intent."

"Damn, you talk funny!" Cantrell said, but some of his anger had flown away. He scowled as he took stock of the dying girl and the three outlaws. "She was a good un'.

Made me lots of money. And *you* boys...I oughta shoot you m'self, save the law from wastin' time tyin' nooses for your three worthless necks!"

"What Mr. Lawson fails to realize," Mathias said in his calm and oily voice, "is that *four* nooses will have to be made ready in Cheyenne. Eric James rode with us for many months of his own free will. He's not exactly an *innocent*. I imagine he's realized that...and he knows he can't ever go home again, so he's likely gone straight to our cabin to break open my strongbox. Get himself enough money for the train and a new life in San Francisco, and to hell with the doctor and this wench."

"What's he talkin' about?" Cantrell asked.

"Eric could've left here anytime he pleased," Mathias went on, directing his comments to Lawson. "I wasn't keeping him locked up."

"Maybe not *him* locked up, but I think he probably had no way to get money for the trip unless he *did* break open your strongbox. And you were not going to let him or either of these two very far from your sight, were you? No trust or honor among thieves and killers, am I correct?"

Blue moaned. Ann was kneeling at her side. "She's in a bad way," Ann said. "Where's that damn doctor?"

"He's not coming," said Mathias. "Eric's gone for the money."

"Bleedin' all over my floor," Cantell muttered. "New boards and all!"

The whistle blew again, maybe announcing an intention to pull out early. Lawson said, "Nealsen, I'll pay you ten dollars to go to the station and hold that train for twenty minutes. Ann, would you get our bags packed and put aboard?"

"I will," she said, and hurriedly left the Palace. Nealsen looked for permission from Cantrell, who said, "I wouldn't mind earnin' ten my own self, but go on. Tell Tabbers to do what you say because *I'm* sayin' it."

Nealsen left, also in a hurry.

"Mind if I have a drink while we wait for Eric James not to come back with the doctor?" Mathias asked.

"I do. Stand where you are."

"Blood on my boots!" said Cantrell. "*Sheeeeyit*!"

Not fifteen seconds later the canvas was whipped aside and in came a slender wisp of a man, about fifty years of age, with sad eyes and a sallow complexion. He wore spectacles and a stained brown overcoat and carried a doctor's bag. Snowflakes clung to his gray hair and powdered the shoulders of his coat. Behind him came Eric Cavanaugh, the sight of which brought forth a dry chuckle and a shake of the head from Deuce Mathias.

"Swore you weren't coming back, Eric," said Mathias. "*I* wouldn't have been so stupid."

The doctor at once knelt down beside Blue. The joints of his knees popped. It took him hardly a moment before he said, with what Lawson thought was a Scandinavian accent, "It's bad. Let's get her up on the bar, *ya*?"

"And smear blood all over my bartop?" Cantrell's temper flared again. "Hell no, Fossie, leave her where she is!"

"Up on the bar," the doctor repeated, with admirable grace under pressure. "*Now*," he insisted.

"You two." Lawson motioned at Mathias and Presco with the Colt's business end. "Do it, *quick*."

"I don't think we will," came the half-jeering reply. "You won't—"

The vampire slapped Mathias across the face so hard with his free hand that the man's eyes almost burst from his head. It was just a fraction of Lawson's strength, and he was hardpressed to hold back so as not to rip the melon from its stalk. At full tilt, when he had to, Lawson could likely knock down a horse or kick a stagecoach onto its side, thus even the small matter of shaking a man's hand was a challenge.

A thread of blood drooled from Mathias's lower lip. He was going to have a black bruise in the shape of a hand on his right cheek and his right eye would be swelling shut. The smell of this new blood did nothing for Lawson's disposition. He grabbed a handful of Mathias's hair, jerked the head back and nearly shoved the Colt's barrel up a nostril. Pure terror put a gleam of phantom light in the man's eyes.

"Yes sir, movin'," said Keene Presco. The rusty saw-blade voice skreeched and scratched. "Movin', sir." He was already bending down to get Blue's legs.

Lawson put his face right in Mathias's. He let the man get a close glimpse of the vampire, as if releasing that most vile part of himself for just an instant. He knew the crimson cat-shine at the center of his eyes and the briefest impression of a lower jaw thrusting forward to unhinge itself would be enough. He added, in a nearly inaudible whisper, "*There are worse thingsssss than death.*"

The next sound was that of liquid spattering onto Mathias's boots. Lawson could smell the beer in it.

The man shuddered. Tears surfaced in his eyes. For some reason Lawson doubted this man had cried since he was six years old. Lawson released him, and Mathias made a whimpering sound and scurried over to help Presco.

When Blue was up on the bar the doctor went to work, opening his bag and bringing out wads of cotton and a pair of wicked-looking forceps. The wound was visible above the gown's neckline, which was gore-soaked and no longer anywhere near blue. The doctor checked her heartbeat with a stethoscope. Blue began to moan again, and her body trembled and shivered. Her hands came up to claw at the bullet-hole.

"Keep her hands down, please," said Fossie, whose real name Lawson figured was a Nordic jawbreaker. Without being asked Mathias and Presco did the job.

"What about *me*?" Johnny Rebinaux called from his slumped posture on the floor. His accent was grits-and-cornbread Southern. South Georgia, Lawson figured. "I'm bleedin' to death over here, ain't nobody gonna hep' me?"

"Someone pour me a big glass of whiskey. Strongest you've got, *ya*?" said the doctor, Cantrell went behind the bar and obliged, pouring a glass from a fresh bottle labelled Black Lightning. Fossie soaked a wad of cotton in the dark caramel-colored potion and cleaned the wound as much as he could. Blue was thankfully out once more and made no sound. Then Fossie put the forceps in the whiskey.

"This pain may cause her to come around. I'm going to probe for the bullet. It's so near her heart...yet her heartbeat is still strong, for the moment. Hold her, please."

Eric moved in to help. Which was good, because in the next few seconds as the forceps entered the wound Blue began to buck and fight with extraordinary strength. It took all of Mathias, Presco and Eric to keep her down. Though Blue's eyes were still closed the trauma of pain wracked her face, causing the muscles to jump in her cheeks and jaw. Fossie worked with a careful and patient hand, silent in his concentration.

"Can you find it?" Eric asked, but Fossie didn't reply.

At last the bloody forceps was withdrawn from the wound. It was empty.

Blue stopped fighting. She lay still, but she yet drew her breath in shallow whispers.

"The bullet," said Fossie, "is lodged beside the right atrium. I can't get hold of it without causing further damage."

"But you *can* remove it in your surgery, can't you?" Lawson asked.

"My *surgery?*" Fossie gave him a crooked and rather sad smile. "My *barn,* would be a better description. My efforts are limited by my circumstances and surroundings, sir. Not only does she need a surgical specialist, she needs a transfusion of blood. I don't have the instruments or facilities for such procedures."

"What are you saying? You're giving up on her?"

Fossie pushed his spectacles up on his nose with a bloody finger. "Sir, it's a wonder she's still alive. Although…I would give her only a few hours before her heart…as a layman would say…gives out."

"Then *do* something! The best you can!"

"My best," the doctor replied, "would be to pack the wound, go to the telegraph office and inform the hospital at Helena that a female gunshot victim is on the way. They would have a medical wagon ready at the station."

"The station?" Lawson was usually as sharp as a new razor, but all this perfume of gore in the air had him dazed.

"Of course. The road from here to Helena would be impassible."

"All right. You'll take her?"

"I cannot. There's nothing more I can do for her except keep her sleeping. And to leave here...what if I'm needed by someone I can actually *help*? No, I'm sorry. I can't take her."

"But *we* can, Mr. Lawson," said Eric. "The train's going to Helena. They can meet us with the wagon as soon as we get there."

Lawson had already considered this. It was the right thing to do, but the blood smell...it taunted him, it stirred the restless and horrifying currents within him, it made him *want* to drink, made him want to...

As LaRouge had told him, in the half-flooded mansion in Nocturne...*learn to be a god.*

Lawson lowered his face. He feared that his desires were showing, and also his struggle.

"If she's going to live until morning," Fossie said, "she'll have to get to that hospital."

"What about *me*?" Rebinaux squalled. "My hand ain't worth a Yankee's promise!"

"Stop whining," the doctor told him. "There's nothing wrong with you a bonesaw won't cure."

"We've got to get her where she needs to go," said Eric, speaking to his savior. "Forget these three. We can't let her die!"

Lawson looked up from the blood and the sawdust, because it was time for a decision. "You're right. But forget these three? No. Doctor, will you send the telegraph message?"

"I will. First..." He turned his attention to Eric. "Jacob's closed his store by now. Go get him. Tell him we need two blankets and something to carry her on. He might have a stretcher, I don't know. Tell him to put it on my bill."

"Yes sir," said Eric, and he was off again.

"I'll pack her wound and then I'll see to you," Fossie told Rebinaux. "Make any more noise and I may have to cut off a few fingers."

"Take off your gunbelts," Lawson said to Mathias and Presco. "Drop them *easy*. Then sit down at that table and be still." He pointed with his Colt where he wanted them to settle, and they obeyed him as if indeed he already had reached godhood, or something nearly like it. Deuce Mathias kept staring at the floor and running his hands over his face as if trying to wake himself up from a bad dream.

By the time Fossie had finished what he could do for Blue and bound Rebinaux's mangled hand with bandages, Eric was back with the blankets and a short ladder. Under Lawson's command, the two desperadoes set Blue on the ladder, the doctor folded a blanket behind her head and smoothed the other one over her, Rebinaux hauled himself up from the floor cursing all the way and they were ready to go.

"Here," Fossie set before they started out. He brought a small brown bottle from his bag and offered it to Lawson. "She shouldn't wake before you reach Helena, but if she does and she fights to get at that wound, put some of this down her throat. It's morphine and straight rotgut whiskey, enough to drop a mule." Then the doctor's eyes narrowed behind his spectacles. "You are also ill, Mr. Lawson?"

"I've been better," said the vampire. "I will be again."

The doctor nodded, though Lawson was certainly sure Fossie had no idea what illness he was looking at. Lawson ordered Mathias and Presco to carry the girl between them. Johnny Rebinaux staggered along. Eric and the doctor followed them out and through the throng that had gathered outside in the falling snow, while Cantrell stayed behind to make sure his Palace wasn't looted.

Under the single siding at the small train depot, the 4-4-0 locomotive hissed and seethed as if angered at the delay. The engine would be pulling the same load down from Perdition as it had pulled up: a coal tender, a passenger car and four freight cars. The train's crew of engineer, fireman and conductor had been here since the late afternoon run, likely having their dinner at one of Perdition's two cafes after turning the train southward again on the oval track that circled the town. Nealsen and Ann were waiting on the platform, along with the engineer who Lawson figured was the man Cantrell had referred to as "Tabbers". The gent appeared to be a true Viking, standing about six-foot-three with a flame-red beard and a face that could scare a gargoyle. The fireman, a young black man, was at his station in the cab. Alongside Tabbers stood the conductor, who Lawson and Ann had already seen on the way up; he was a short bulldog of a man about sixty years of age, wearing a dark blue coat and cap, with long white hair flowing about his shoulders and the battered look of a boxer who had gone a few rounds too many.

Fossie went directly into the telegraph office to send the message. "Get her aboard!" the conductor said in nearly a growl when he saw the two men carrying the wounded girl, and he hooked a thumb toward the passenger car. "Everybody else who ain't got a ticket for Helena, get one now and be quick about it!"

Ann had already secured the tickets and put their bags aboard. Lawson paid the bartender the ten dollars he'd promised. Tabbers was climbing up into the engine and the conductor went up the metal steps into the passenger car, which was lit within by oil lamps set in gimbals on the walls. It was time to get started.

But Lawson staggered; he had been holding himself tight against the smell of all this blood, and now he lost himself for an instant. In that terrible span of time the evil desires of the vampire rose up from the place he'd been forcing it down. Not only did the muscles of his face jump and twitch as his mouth seemed to want to open involuntarily, but he saw in the redseared eye of his mind himself slaughtering everyone on this platform—Ann included—and feasting as was his power and right as a god of the night upon these pathetic creatures. Such weaklings as they were did not deserve to live in the world that was to come, and indeed would eventually fall to the fangs of the Dark Society. Why not now? Why not take them all, right this moment? It would be a blessing for them to be released from their hopeless shells, really; he could turn Ann if he pleased. He could set her right with her sister and her father, and she would know what it was like to be chosen...to be fearless...to be a power that no human could resist...

"Are you all right?" Ann asked him, and Lawson saw that he was the center of attention because he had fallen against the wooden wall of the telegraph office and seemed to be hanging there on the verge of toppling to the boards.

He put a hand to his forehead. Usually he was so cold, but tonight he felt feverish.

"Get everyone on the train," he said. "I'll be there in a minute."

"What's the—"

"Just do it. Please."

She nodded. Her face was grim, her lips tight. She well aware that something was going on with him that perhaps she didn't wish to know. Quickly, she turned away and with her gun drawn she oversaw the carrying of Blue into the passenger car. Rebinaux went in, and behind him went Eric. Ann started to speak again to Lawson but when she looked back she saw him stagger into a narrow alley between the telegraph office and the small structure where the tickets were sold. She decided that for the moment there was nothing she could do for him; he would come when he was ready. She went into the passenger car and closed the door behind her.

In the alley, as the snowflakes whirled down and the bitter wind sang, the vampire sought his bottle of cattle blood. He was shamed to his soul for the images and thoughts that had assailed him. But even so, some deep and dark part of him kept whispering *Why not? Why not?*

HE GOT HIS back against the timbers and fumbled for a few seconds with getting the bottle uncorked. His hands, usually so strong, had become as white-fleshed jelly. He was losing control of himself in all ways...physically, mentally, spiritually. The road of no return beckoned him...a horrible road, but one of great beauty too...no, no...not beautiful...a torment, a death-in-life...but what is your life now, Lawson?

He drank from the Japanese bottle. Drained it dry. Still he burned, and still he yearned.

Something scuttled in the alley.

It took him two seconds to focus upon the gray rat that was feasting upon a scattering of garbage in the snow. What was in that pile of refuse was difficult to say, but even to one of vampiric nature it was repulsive.

Blood flowed within the rodent. That was all Lawson needed to know.

He was on the rat in a blur of motion. It was picked up before it realized it was in danger. The desperate creature who gripped it opened his mouth to tear the rat's head off and drink the fluids in a fountain of gore from the ragged neck.

"Mr. Lawson?"

Someone behind him, in the alley.

He froze, standing in the falling snow with the squirming rat right at his mouth, the small claws struggling for purchase, the red eye a bloody cup of terror.

"Mr. Lawson? *Sir?*"

It was the doctor. Lawson would've sensed him there, but all his powers and energies had been aimed toward feeding this ungodly hunger.

He dropped his hand. The rat gave him a little nip on the index finger as it jumped free. No ichor rose;

the rodent's teeth had not gone deep enough. The little scratch would be healed in a few minutes. The rat scrabbled into a tangle of broken crates and was gone.

He turned toward Fossie, who stood about ten feet away at the alley's entrance. If the doctor had seen what he was about to do, what of it?

Take him, the vampire thought. *Do it quickly...*

Fossie cleared his throat. Snowflakes were stuck on the lenses of his spectacles. "I...have sent the message. The train's moving out. You should be on it, *ya*?"

They stared at each other in silence for a few seconds.

Then Lawson nodded.

"Yes, I should be," he answered, and when he approached Fossie the doctor drew back. Maybe he'd seen nothing, maybe he'd seen everything; at the moment Lawson cared not.

The train's whistle gave a shriek and the bell clanged. The wheels were moving...slowly at first, grinding across the rails. White steam hissed from beneath the engine and coal smoke and cinders were beginning to plume from the flared bonnet stack. The big whale-oil headlamp was burning in its protective red tin box mounted just in front of the stack, and leading the engine was a badly-dented cowcatcher that looked as if it had already dispatched a few buffalo to their happy grazing grounds. In the cab the engineer stood at his controls and the black fireman was shovelling coal into the engine's burning maw like he himself was a well-oiled machine.

As Lawson reached for the handrail to pull himself up the steps to the passenger car's front platform, Fossie called out over the increasing noise of the moving wheels and song of steam. He said, "Whatever your illness is...good luck to you."

Lawson did not answer nor look again at the doctor. He went into the passenger car, closed the door at his back, and set eyes first upon the thin, rigid figure of Eli Easterly seated to his left. The man wore a Bible-black suit with a white shirt and a black string-tie. His face and hair were nearly the same shade of gray. Beside him on the slatted wooden seat was a brown leather suitcase, worn by years of wanderings. Their eyes met, but very quickly Easterly shifted his expressionless gaze to watch the last lamps of Perdition slide past.

Lawson wondered what Easterly would think if he knew the vampire's Eye—the flaming orb that entered a human mind and revealed all—had shown him on the train trip up from Helena that this individual had killed at least ten men, had fallen upon the salvation of whiskey and God in equal doses, had become a travelling preacher for years to atone for his sins of wife-beating, whoremongering, and murder in the name of bounty hunting, and had been in Perdition to visit the grave of his only son, shot in the back two months ago and laid to rest in a muddy field along with all the other sons and daughters.

It was a terrible dark justice that claimed the innocent, Lawson thought, because the Eye had shown him that nearly all of those men Easterly had killed were shot in the back.

The whistle blew again, a mournful sound. Snow whirled past the windows. Lawson smelled the rich perfume of Blue's blood, and he wondered how in the name of Christ he was going to make these thirty long miles.

Five.

LAWSON PASSED ELI EASTERLY AND looked for a place to settle himself where he could close his eyes and try to mentally escape this confinement. They had set the ladder with Blue upon it down in the aisle between the seats, toward the rear of the car. Blue was still unconscious, a blanket supporting her head and the second tucked in around her. The bulldog conductor was standing over her, one hand braced against a seat and the other checking his pocketwatch to see how much time they'd lost. Ann sat in the seat ahead, her pistol on the slats uncocked but within quick reach. Mathias, Presco and Rebinaux sat on the other side of the aisle in varying stages of sullen resignation, though

Mathias—having gotten a fearsome glimpse of something, he knew not what—kept a hand clasped over his eyes as if in terror of seeing it again, and he muttered to himself so much that his former cohorts in crime glanced at him as one might take in a pitiful wretch whose mind had crumbled.

Lawson sat down on the seat facing Eric, who had distanced himself by several rows from the others.

"Thank you," the young man said. "I never would've—"

"Keep your voice down," said Lawson, as quietly as possible over the rumble of the wheels. "What I have to say to you I don't want anyone else hearing."

"All right. What is it?"

"I want to know...did you ever *try* to get back home?"

"I couldn't. I had no money of my own, so I couldn't get very far even if I *did* get away. Mathias watched us all like a hawk and kept everything in his strongbox...and I have to tell you, we're leaving about eight thousand dollars behind in that cabin."

"Does Fossie know where the cabin is?"

"Maybe. It wouldn't be hard for him to find. Why?"

"Your gang just bought the doctor a suitable office and surgery for the next person who needs it. I'll telegraph him from Helena to let him know. You'll of course tell me where the cabin is and where the strongbox is kept. Agreed?"

"Sure, but I wouldn't doubt that Cantrell won't try to find it first, knowing it's there to be found."

"Will he find it?"

"Not unless he pulls up the floorboards under Mathias's cot. But he'll have to break the box open. The key's in Deuce's pocket right now."

"It won't take us long to get to Helena," Lawson said. "The telegraph office is right there at the station." He leaned closer toward the young man. His senses were keen; he could smell the blood flowing through Eric's veins. "Another thing," he went on. "Listen to me carefully." He paused for a few seconds to make sure he had Eric's full attention. "In Helena you're going to go with the girl on the hospital wagon. I'm going to give you three hundred dollars. You won't be travelling to Cheyenne with the others. You'll catch a train from Helena to Omaha as soon as you can and you'll go home. Are you hearing me?"

Eric didn't answer quickly enough. Lawson repeated with some force behind it: "Are you *hearing* me?"

"I am," Eric said. He stared out the window beside him, at the darkness that spat snow against the dirty glass. The train was curving, probably going through a mountain pass. "I thank you for getting me out of there," he said. "I will go home...but you don't know what it's like, living with my father. And my two brothers...both of them hung the moon, he thinks. I, on the other hand, am a maker of mud pies. I suppose he told you all about me."

"Enough to know you've made some damn bad choices."

"I didn't choose to be born to this family. I didn't choose to be different from my brothers. To want to live for anything but work, and stepping on people in the name of commerce and *politics*." He spoke that last word as if it were a fatal disease. "To want adventure... freedom from the kind of life that's chained them both down so they can't take a piss without asking his permission. Oh, and they had to marry into the *right* families. Well, I'm *made* that way, Mr. Lawson. I'm made to turn my back on everything my father thinks is holy, because I'm telling you...I don't fit in his church."

Lawson nodded. He understood the young man's point, but that was not why he was here doing this job. "I was paid to get you out of Perdition and aimed toward home. I'm also keeping you out of jail...possibly prison, or worse if Mathias could convince a judge you killed someone. Which I'm not sure you haven't. But look at me and listen very closely, Eric...it's not up to me whether you stay in Omaha, in your father's house, or wherever. It is up to me to make *certain* you do at least go see your father. Then you can go and do as you please. But...you *are* going to Omaha, and you *are* going to see him. If you don't, I'll hear about it." Lawson settled back against the hard slats. "I won't like hearing that you've disobeyed me, after what Ann and I have done. I'll track you from Helena if I have to, and I'll find you. So do me the favor of time and yourself the favor of mercy, and at least let your father see his son."

Eric kept his gaze directed out the window. He drew a long breath and released it, and from that action of resignation Lawson understood that Eric had been thinking of catching a train in Helena for anywhere but Omaha.

"I'll go see him," Eric said at last. "I won't promise I'll stay there a whole day."

"As you please. My business with you and your father is concluded when you set eyes upon each other. I wasn't contracted to be your guardian angel."

"Fair enough," the young man agreed.

Ann suddenly said, "Lawson! She's coming around!"

At once Lawson was on his feet and walking back along the car toward where Blue lay. Ann was kneeling at her side and the conductor was standing over her. He moved aside to let Lawson kneel down. The aroma of dried blood in the packed wound hit Lawson with a force that no one else in the car could possibly understand. His face tightened. His lower jaw wanted to unhinge and the fangs to slide out from the upper. The images of destroying everyone here in a fury of insane greed wanted to further unhinge the iron door of the crypt he carried with him to protect weak humans just like these.

Blue's eyes fluttered. She was as pallid as death, and already she looked to Lawson as she might if she were turned...and yet, if she were turned she would never need worry about lead bullets again. They might hurt, but they could never kill.

"*Water,*" Blue whispered.

A leather-covered canteen was offered from an age-spotted hand with crooked knuckles.

Lawson took it. He unscrewed the cap and as gently as possible put the canteen to Blue's lips. She was able to drink just a little, but most ran down her chin. Lawson handed the canteen back. "Thank you," he said.

"Sorry she's in such a bad way," said the conductor. He returned the canteen to a shelf above where he usually sat. "Which one of them fellas shot her?"

"The one who used to have a gunhand," Ann said.

"Somebody talkin' about me?" Rebinaux spoke up. "Hell, ain't my fault Deuce pushed her! I weren't aimin' to shoot no saloon girl!"

"But you did," the conductor answered. "I ought to come over there and knock a few teeth outta that dumb-lookin' face."

"Come on then, pappy!" Rebinaux started to get out of his seat. He was grinning like a pure fool but there was meanness in his mouth. "I'll bust yore ass with one gotdamn hand!"

"Sit down." Mathias reached up and took hold of Rebinaux's jacket sleeve. The man's voice was a weak ghost of what it had been at the first of the evening. "There's no point in that, Johnny."

Rebinaux jerked away. His cheeks had reddened and his overhanging brow seemed even lower than a few seconds before. "No point? No *point*? Hell, we're all bound for Mexican neckties and we're sittin' here doin' *nothin'*? Jesus eatin' hominy, Deuce! You're supposed to be lookin' out for us! In the old days we'd storm this bunch and turn 'em guts-side out! We'd take this whole damn train over! And look at us, Keene!" he said to his other companion, trying to pull him into this fray. "We're the saddest sacks ever sittin' in shitty britches!" Presco responded by staring at the floorboards. "Well," Rebinaux raved on, "you can both go all hangy-dog but at least I can knock a damn old man into next week!"

"Come on yourself, sweetpea!" The conductor smiled, though his face was also blooming red and his white eyebrows were dancing. He turned to fully face his adversary. His hands had become fists, and he planted his feet like a man who would not be moved. "One wallop from Glorious George Gantt and your head'll be on the moon 'fore mornin'!"

"Sit down," Mathias repeated.

"Seems we ought to clean house startin' with that *punk*!" Rebinaux showed his bad green teeth at Eric Cavanaugh. "I told you we shouldn't oughta take him on! Look what he's brung us!"

"Sit down, Dixie," said the vampire. He stood up and drew back his coat to show his two guns. Of course no one but Ann knew that the Colt with the grip of yellowed bone, sitting backwards in Lawson's holster on his left side, was loaded with six silver bullets blessed with holy water by Father John Deale. The silver angels could kill a human, yes, but they were meant to penetrate the skull of a member of the Dark Society and in so doing burn the creature's body to a fine ash. Within Lawson's coat was a derringer that also carried two of the consecrated bullets. "*Down*," he repeated, putting a hand on the pistol with the rosewood grip.

"You ain't gonna shoot an unarmed man!" Rebinaux spat back. "You ain't got the stones for that!"

"You and I measure courage in different ways. Ann, which ear should I take off?"

"Gentlemen," said a hollow voice. "*Please*."

Eli Easterly had risen to his feet. He came along the aisle slowly, and though the train was moving at a good clip now and the car was rocking a few degrees back and forth he kept his balance well, not needing to touch any seatback as he passed. He positioned himself between Lawson and Rebinaux. "I have no idea what's transpired here," he said, "but violence is never an answer." His sad gray eyes in the gray face under the gray but carefully-combed hair were fixed upon Lawson. "You're an intelligent man. You understand the futility of violence."

"I understand it's sometimes unfortunately necessary."

"Perhaps. But I doubt it's necessary to deprive anyone present of an ear." He turned his head toward Rebinaux. "You should sit down, sir. God is in this place. He will protect, if you allow Him."

"I don't need protection! I need a damn horse and two hours head start!"

Easterly nodded. "Even so," he said quietly.

The moment hung. Then Rebinaux made a farting sound with his mouth toward Glorious George Gantt. He said, "You can all go straight to Hell and roast your nuts! You too, lady! And you *most* of all, ya coward!" After making this statement to Deuce Mathias he staggered across the aisle and sat by himself on a seat toward the front.

Easterly came forward a few more paces to look down upon Blue, who was making small whimpering sounds but appeared to be for the most part unconscious again. "Wound near the heart," he said. "She's lost a lot of blood."

"She has," Lawson answered.

"Dr. Fossenhurst couldn't remove the bullet?"

"No. We're taking her to the hospital in Helena."

"And these men?"

"Bound for Cheyenne. Wanted for crimes in the territory."

"Ah. You and the young lady are the law?"

"In a way."

A faint smile pulled at the corners of the man's mouth, but his eyes remained cold. "I thought I recognized you for what you are on the trip up. I've seen many of your kind, but this is the first time I've met a *female* bounty hunter." He gave Ann a slight nod.

"We have a job to do." Lawson decided not to try to correct the man as to their true mission. "We intend to do it with no further violence. About Dr. Fossenhurst... are you a friend of his?"

"Not exactly. He wrote a letter to me informing me of..." The gray eyes blinked, and the faint smile was gone. "A tragedy in my family."

"I'm very sorry, Mr. Easterly," Lawson said, and immediately he realized what mistake the need for blood and all this aroma of gore had done to his senses.

Eli Easterly's face remained blank. His head cocked slightly to one side, as if he were trying to puzzle out exactly what he was looking at. "I don't recall telling you my name," he said.

"Didn't you?" Lawson asked, himself feeling as if his world was rapidly spinning out of control.

"No, I did not."

"Surely you—"

"*No.*" Easterly's right hand slid into his coat. It emerged again holding a small unornamented silver crucifix, which he clasped to his chest. "It's *Reverend* Easterly," he said, and Lawson felt the drawing of some sharp blade between them. Red embers of a fire had begun to ignite deep in the man's eyes. Lawson thought *He doesn't know, but he senses—*

There was sudden jolt that made Easterly stumble backward and grip the seatback beside him. The jolt brought a squall from Johnny Rebinaux. Ann staggered into Lawson, but the vampire held steady.

The train's wheels shrieked, an ungodly sound. The timbers of the passenger car groaned as if in mortal pain.

"Christ Almighty!" Gantt hollered over the noise. He had nearly been pitched to his knees.

In struggling to keep his balance, Easterly lost the crucifix. It hit the floor with a metallic chime a few inches from Lawson's right boot.

The train was slowing. Steam bellowed from beneath the engine and for an instant whitened out the windows. Then it had cleared and again there was just the night and the blowing snow. The train continued to lose speed, the wheels still screaming, and then...

"Why are we stopping?" Lawson asked Gantt.

"Hell if I know!" was the growled reply. "Either Tabbers or Rooster up there must be sittin' on that brake!"

Another few seconds, and the train came to a dead standstill after a last little backward jolt and burst of steam.

"What's this about?" Deuce Mathias was on his feet. He'd regained some of his composure and spirit, but still dared not look at the pallid and very fearsome man with the two Colts in his holster.

"Heh!" Rebinaux shouted. "Betcha we're gettin' robbed! There's some mighty evil men hereabouts!" He slammed his good hand against the seat in front of him. "Deuce, we can still get out of this!"

"Shut up, Johnny!" Presco hollered in his rusty-saw-blade voice. "Just shut your hole!"

"Everyone, quiet!" Lawson commanded. He saw Easterly's crucifix on the floor. Though the sight of it made his eyes water and burn he was not so far gone that he was compelled to flee from it in shame and anguish, but it had been a very long time since he'd touched one of those. He started to reach down for it and hesitated.

Would it burn his fingers? Could he stand to touch it, even now in this early stage of the transition? He feared it, because it meant he might be discovered as something both more and less than human.

"Would you pick that up for me, please?" Easterly asked, standing a few feet away.

The vampire's hand was still outstretched, but the truth was...he was afraid, and now he understood how the older ones would shield their eyes and their flesh from the power of this object. Why it was so—why his eyes burned at the sight and why his skin and senses shrank from it—he did not know, just as he didn't fully understand why the silver bullets blessed with holy water could destroy the vampires so decisively. These were mysteries of the constant battle between light and darkness that he had recognized were far beyond him.

"Here," Ann said, as she picked up the crucifix and offered it to Easterly.

The reverend took it, pressed it between both hands against his chest again, and directed his sharp-edged gaze to Lawson when he said, "Thank you kindly."

"Stopped out here in the middle of nowhere!" Gantt fumed. He had spent a few seconds igniting a lantern from the tinderbox he carried. "Lemme go see what Tabber's up to!" He pushed past Ann and Lawson and gave Rebinaux a disdainful glare just before he left the car. Opening the door brought in a swirl of snow and made Ann shiver and pull her coat's collar up around her neck.

Lawson suddenly felt it.

Not the frigid cold, nor the sting of ice in the wind. Those didn't bother him. What he felt in the air was a venomous presence, a sensation of massed power coiling itself for a strike. It seemed to curl itself around his throat, lay claws upon his shoulders and whisper a foul enticement in his ear. He felt himself shiver as Ann had, for he knew what must be true: out there, very near, were creatures of the Dark Society.

"Watch them," he told her. "I'm going up front."

"What is it?" she asked, sensing his tension.

"Maybe nothing," he replied, but they both knew better.

He left the passenger car and stepped down to the ground. His boots sank in the crust of snow and ice. The wind had picked up and was blowing hard. He tied the leather chinstrap of his Stetson into place. Snow whirled around him and ice crystals stung his cheeks. It was a night fit for neither man nor beast, but Lawson figured it suited *them* just right.

He saw Gantt's shape and the glow of the lantern ahead as the man approached the locomotive's cab, and he started walking toward it. The engine was still throbbing steam. Lawson was aware of mountains on both sides of the track: huge chunks of snow-covered rock that pulsed faintly blue in the vampire's night-vision. Boulders seemed to hang several hundred feet overhead, for the train had stopped in a narrow pass. Lawson guessed they were maybe seven or eight miles south of Perdition, and there was not a light of habitation to be seen.

As Lawson approached, Gantt was aiming his lantern upward at Tabbers and the black fireman the conductor had called Rooster.

"Go on!" Tabbers was saying. "Take a look for yourself!"

"*Damn it*!" Gantt had almost jumped out of his boots as he realized Lawson was standing beside him. His white hair was blown wildly about his shoulders by the wind, and he was holding onto his dark blue cap with his free hand. "Friend, I don't like to be sneaked up on!"

"My apologies. What's happened?"

"Track's blocked," said the red-bearded Viking, who was bundled up in a long brown leather coat and wore black cloth gloves. "About forty yards ahead. We nearly crashed our asses into it before we saw it. Rooster before me...the boy's got better eyes."

"Jesus Christ!" Gantt made a face like he wanted to spit acid. "Let's take a gander!" He started off walking alongside the steaming locomotive and Lawson followed just behind him. They reached the front end of the engine and saw, illuminated through the snowfall by the cone of the big whale-oil headlamp, that the track was indeed blocked by a pile of boulders and smaller rocks nearly the height of a man.

"Lord lord lord," said the conductor, as if chanting a dirge. "Look at that mess! Must've happened not too long ago...snow's not piled up on the rocks yet." He made a sucking noise through his teeth. "Well…we got pickaxes and shovels aboard. Have to put everybody to work who can. It'll be a hell of a job. You want to go fetch 'em while I take a closer look, Mr. Lawson?"

"Don't do that," said the vampire.

"Pardon?"

They were here, watching. Lawson felt them, hiding in the crevices and holes, flattened against the earth, crouched amid the twisted leafless trees. They were waiting, and how long they'd been waiting here he did not know. Their web of communications was yet not fully understood by him, but he knew they tracked him, waiting for a moment just like this.

"Can this engine move in reverse?" he asked.

"It can. Or…it could, if you didn't care that the railcars were busted into splinters. Have to decouple the cars, and that ain't gonna happen tonight." Gantt lifted his lantern to examine Lawson's face. The vampire quickly averted his eyes so the lamp would pick up no gleam of red. "What do you mean, *don't do that*? We've got to get this line cleared!"

"I mean…don't go out there."

"And why the hell *not*?"

Lawson turned his gaze upon the man, and cared not if the red glint scared the piss out of him. At that moment he wanted to.

"You won't come back," said Lawson.

"*Huh*? Are you—" And then something in Lawson's face or voice must've gotten through, because Gantt lowered the lantern and stood staring toward the pile of boulders. The cruel wind blew snow into his face, like a taunt. "That girl," Gantt said after a moment. "She'll die if you don't get her to Helena." It was a statement, for there was no question about it.

"Yes," was the answer. Lawson was beginning to think that was a terrible word.

"So then, why—"

"Walk with me back to the cab. Go on, quickly."

Lawson waited for Gantt to go first.

As they left the front of the engine some small object came flying from the darkness with tremendous speed and shattered the glass of the headlamp. Its force was enough to take it into the fuel well. Burning whale-oil spewed out and drooled down in tendrils of blue flame upon the cowcatcher.

With that, the lamp flickered…flickered…and went dark.

"My light!" Tabbers shouted as he leaned down from the cab. "Jumpin' Jaysus! What happened to my light?"

Lawson ignored him. There were worse things to contend with than a sightless eye. "Do you have guns?"

"*What*?"

"Guns. Firearms. *Anything*. Do you have them?"

"We…got two rifles. Why?"

"Loaded?"

"No, but—"

"Load them," said the vampire. "*Now.*"

Six.

"**YOU CAN'T BE TELLIN'** *ME* what to do, fella!" Tabbers fired back. "Who the hell do you think you are?"

"I'm the man trying to keep you and everyone else here alive tonight. When you get your rifles loaded, come back to the passenger car. Keep your heads on swivels and move fast." Lawson told Gantt, "Come with me," and the conductor did not hesitate.

Back in the passenger car and the welcome yellow light of the oil lamps, the first voice upraised belonged to Johnny Rebinaux. "Why we stopped, bossman? Bandits or Injuns?"

"What's going on, Lawson?" Mathias dared asked.

Reverend Easterly had returned to his seat and silently watched as Lawson walked along the aisle to check on Blue. "She was making a whimpering sound a minute ago," Ann told him. "Tried to get her hands on the wound, but I kept them down. She's out again, it looks like." Ann's fierce black eyes asked the question first, then her voice, speaking quietly: "They're here?"

That word again. "Yes."

"Trevor, how did they *find* us?"

"They tracked us, in their way. Maybe they had a human spy watching us. Could be it's like some telegraph system that ordinary humans can't fathom. And I can't fathom it either...not yet."

"Is something wrong with the engine, Mr. Lawson?" Eric asked.

"Nothin' wrong with that," said Gantt, who hung his lantern up on a nail for the moment. The stricken expression on Gantt's face told Lawson the conductor still didn't know what to make of the headlamp being broken out. "The rail's blocked. There's been a rockslide."

"Ha!" Rebinaux's ugly grin widened. "Deuce, listen to me! We can get out of this, if we've a mind to! Keene, you up for it?"

"For *what*?" Presco asked. He had his face pressed against a window's glass trying to see past the coal tender and engine, but the snow and the night made it impossible. "Gettin' shot dead right here or froze to death out in that weather? We ain't got a baby's chance in Hell!"

"A baby wouldn't be in Hell, ya jackass!" Rebinaux snarled. "A baby's born without sin, so why's a baby gonna be in Hell? Yeah, I always figured there was some yellow on that belly!"

Presco's fuse had finally been lit. He stood up and lumbered like an angry bear into the aisle. "Fine talk you're doin', Johnny!" he shouted in a voice that sounded like a room full of saws working rusted metal. "And you with one hand! You can't do nothin'!"

"I can kick you where you used to have balls!" Rebinaux hollered back, but he made no move to give action to that threat.

"Settle down!" Lawson took a few paces forward to get between them if he needed to, but he quickly saw that Rebinaux's courage was in trying to get others to risk their skins for him. "Take it easy, Presco. Nobody's going anywhere right now."

"A baby in Hell!" Rebinaux wasn't done needling his ex-partner. "That's just plain dumb!" He snorted as if to get the smell of disgust out of his nostrils.

"Lawson, what did you mean out there?" Gantt came forward along the aisle. "About not comin' back? You think you know somethin' we don't?"

What to tell them? the vampire asked himself. He was thirsty, his nerves on edge, the ichor sluggish in his body. In his bag there were two more bottles of cattle blood, but those were poor substitutes for the rich feast that flowed in a human's veins. His last taste of that had been nearly two months ago, from the throat of a derelict in a tarpaper shack on the banks of the Mississippi. He had left the man alive, but barely. Still...without human blood for more than three months he became a true shade between vampire and man, a scrabbling wretch desperate to feed and gnawed by the knowledge that each feeding from humans took him closer to the edge of the abyss.

They were waiting for him to speak. What to tell them?

There was the sound of boots on the car's front platform. The door opened and from the snow and wind came the black fireman called Rooster. He was likely twenty-four or so, of medium-height and slim build except for a broad back and a formidable set of shoulders. He had a high-cheekboned face with a small, neatly-trimmed goatee and deep-set, cautious eyes. He was wearing a gray woolen coat, a black cap and black gloves and he carried a Winchester rifle.

"Mr. Tabberson didn't come back," Rooster said, as the snow blew around him from the open door. He realized he was letting winter destroy the warmth of the car, so he closed the door behind him. "Mr. Tabberson," he repeated, as snow melted on his shoulders and the brim of his cap. "He went out to them rocks to see. I called him, but he didn't give an answer."

"Why didn't you go help him?" Gantt demanded. "Tabbers maybe fell down, hurt himself."

"I was gonna, but...this fella said to come here after we loaded the rifles. I said, 'Come on, Mr. Tabberson', but he was like... 'Ain't nobody bossin' me on my own train'. So he told me to stay there in the cab, and he took a lamp. I said he shouldn't oughta go, 'cause what had happened to that headlight? He said the tin box must've heated up too fast and the cold broke the glass, and then he went on. After awhile I called him. I used the speakin' trumpet, so he could hear over that wind, but he didn't come back. I was hopin'...a couple of you fellas, and me... we'll go see if he's all right."

"He's not," said Lawson.

"Sir?"

"Did he take a rifle?"

"He did."

"Did you hear any shots?"

"No sir...all that wind...but..." Rooster frowned. "What would he be shootin' at out there?"

"I don't care what you say, Lawson." Gantt lifted the lantern off its nail. "I'm goin' out there to help him, if he needs it. And he *must,* 'cause Tabbers is a tough piece a' leather."

"What's this about the headlight?" Eric asked. "It *broke?*"

"Happens sometimes. Ain't nothin'."

"You know it didn't shatter on its own," said Lawson. "That wasn't just to put out the light. It was a message."

"Do tell!"

"They're telling us they're in control."

"They? *Who*? Indians? The Sioux have cleared out around here! They've—"

"You'll wish they *were* only Indians on the warpath."

"Who, then?"

Again...what to tell them? How to make them understand? Lawson realized that whatever he told them, they were going to think him utterly insane. He looked to Ann for help, but she shook her head because at the moment she knew they'd never believe either of them.

"I think," Eli Easterly suddenly spoke up, "that Mr. Lawson has been dabbling in something...shall we say... *unholy,* and it has come back to bite him."

"What are you jabberin' about?" There was now a twang of fear in the Southern drawl.

"Look at him. Take a good long look. How different he appears from most men. And I noted with interest that he would not dare to touch my crucifix." Easterly stood up into the aisle. "I have seen much in this life. I have known much darkness myself. Therefore I have learned to recognize it." He aimed a finger at the vampire. "This so-called man among us, friends, can only be one thing: a warlock."

"A war*what*?" Presco asked.

"A male witch," Easterly clarified. "Travelling with a female witch, but she's not completely sold to the Devil because she *could* touch the Cross. I had a strange feeling about this man the first time I laid eyes on him. He read my mind and he exudes evil. Can't you feel it, in this car?"

"Yes!" Mathias had nearly shouted it. "Hell, yes! I've *been* feeling it!"

"Oh for God's sake!" said Gantt. "There ain't no such thing as witches!"

"I say this creature before us is…well, just *look* at him! And if he's afraid of something out there that's blocked the track, then you know what that must be? Either one of two things: a rival witch, as dark-souled as himself and his familiar, or…the vengeance and pure white justice of Heaven."

Lawson managed a small, mirthless laugh.

"We're making him nervous, do you see that?" The reverend's finger of accusation was still aimed at Lawson. "He can't bear the light. I noted also—being in the hotel with him and the woman—he never came out during the day. *She* was about, but not he. Oh, no… the light of truth cannot be borne by this creature." Slowly, Easterly's hand fell to his side. "Gentlemen, we are in the presence of an abomination before our Holy Father."

"I think he's just an asshole, m'self!" Rebinaux said.

"Reverend Easterly," Lawson said in a quiet, restrained voice, "you have become...let me say...unsettled by the life you've led. May I call you Eli?" He let that hang for a few seconds. "I am sorry you've lost your only son, Eli. A bullet in the back and a grave in a wretched field. It's been difficult for you, I know. Especially since you sent so many men to their own wretched graves by bullets in the back." He watched as the blood—what paltry amount there was in the man's body—drained from Easterly's face and left him as pale as a vampire's buttocks. "I believe," Lawson continued in the same quiet tone, "that there's a man of good worth still inside you, but he's been hiding for a long time under a bottle and a Bible. Sometimes both at once. I am no warlock, sir, nor is Ann a witch. Though it is true, I have read your mind and I have the ability to read the mind of every man on this train. I would like for you to consider me in our present condition a..." He paused in thought of what his next words would be. Then he recalled something he'd said to Eric just a little while ago. Something he'd said he was not, and now he must recant.

"Consider me your guardian angel," he said, speaking now to all of them. "I'm the best chance you have of...as Mr. Mathias said to me earlier this evening...seeing another sunrise." He looked toward where Blue lay, and his gut twisted...not now for the thirst for her blood, for that was a constant, but for the truth that she would certainly die if action was not taken.

What was she to him? What was anyone in this car to him, but an opportunity to feed, to grow stronger, to revel in his path toward godhood?

"I am Trevor Lawson," he said to the floorboards, and to the silence that was cut only by the wind and to the vampire the sound of beating hearts and lifeblood flowing. "I was born in Alabama. I have…I had a wife and daughter. I fought in the war, at Shiloh. I am a man. I am a man. I am a man." He squeezed his eyes shut for a few seconds. "I swear…that's all I want to be."

When he lifted his head he looked directly at the conductor. "I'll go with you to find Tabbers, but for the sake of your life, stay close to me."

"I'll go," Rooster offered. "Mr. Tabberson been a very good man, I owe him plenty."

"I'll go too," Eric said, but Lawson waved him away. They had not come so far to lose the young man to what lurked out there waiting.

"Load up with silver," Lawson told Ann. "Save your bullets and keep watch on that back door." Then, to the others, "I presume no one will be stupid enough to try to leave this car." He fired a red gleam at the reverend. "Now would be a good time for prayer, concentrating on your own soul," he said. "All right, let's go."

Lawson led the way, with Gantt and his lantern following and Rooster right behind with his rifle. Lawson had the sensation that the rifle was trained at his back most of the way. As they got up alongside the engine, Lawson looked back and told Rooster, "I'm drawing a pistol," so no nervous finger jerked on a Winchester trigger. He smoothly drew the Colt with the grip of yellowed bone. Six silver slugs would finish off six members of the Dark Society, if he was lucky.

If.

They walked along the track, into the wind and snow. Already the pile of boulders and smaller rocks looked to be frozen together. Gantt's light picked out the prints of Tabbers' size-twelve boots, heading around to the right side of the obstruction. A shift of the lantern further to the right showed a rocky decline stubbled with gnarled pine trees, junipers, aspens and a ground covering of sagebrush and greasewood shrubs. Lawson figured this was a perfect place for an ambush, be it from bandits, Indians or other.

"Tabbers!" Gantt shouted. "Tabbers, answer up!"

"Mr. Tabberson!" Rooster called. "Where are you?"

"Don't go any further," Lawson advised when Gantt started to walk around the blockage, and the conductor obeyed without question.

"Tabbers!" Gantt lifted the lantern and swung it back and forth. "We're here, Jack! Answer us!"

Lawson caught a movement to the left, over where the rugged cliffs started to rise. Then there was a movement to the right, down among the pines and the thicket. No one else could have seen these flashes of motion but he, for he knew they were creatures moving at rapid speed from one hiding-place to another. How many had gathered here? His senses told him forty...fifty or more... and not all were of human shape.

He heard a sound at the center of the wind.

"Help...help me...help..."

It was coming from further down the embankment, in amid the underbrush.

"Help...help..."

A pitiful cry, nearly a sob of terror and agony.

"Hear that?" Rooster obviously had good ears as well as good eyes. "Comin' from down there!" He raised his voice to a ragged shout: "Mr. Tabberson! Where are you?"

"Help...please...help..."

"I hear him!" said Gantt. He called out, "Jack, are you hurt?"

The cry for help faded. The wind took it, and it was gone.

"Maybe he's got a broke leg! Took a tumble, that coulda busted his leg!" Rooster was taking measure of a way down the embankment without breaking his own bones. "I gotta get to him!"

"Listen to me!" Lawson put a hand on Rooster's coat collar before the man could start down and held him in an iron grip. "You don't know what's down there! Tabbers is *finished*. Even if they let you get close to him, you wouldn't find him...but they'd have you!"

"Lemme go! Hear me? I said I gotta—"

Rooster pulled to get loose; he was strong, but to the vampire it was like restraining an infant. "You're not going. Neither of you are. I told you…he's finished."

The cry started up again, only now it sounded further to the right and closer.

"Help me…please…help me…"

"They're moving him. Come on, we're getting back inside."

"No sir! No *sir*!" Rooster tried to push Lawson away but it was like one man trying to move the biggest boulder on the track. He said fiercely, "Mr. Tabberson's hurt and he needs help!"

"You can't help him. I can't either. Gantt, start back. You follow him. Go on!" In spite of the Winchester, he gave Rooster a shake when the fireman didn't obey. "I'll carry you if I have to! Or I'll knock the hell out of you first! *Move*!"

"Help…Jesus…help me…"

And again the voice faded away.

The Winchester's barrel went up under Lawson's throat.

Rooster's face was right up in the vampire's, and if he saw anything fearsome at close range to that visage he did not flinch.

"I'll move, Mister Alabama," he said through gritted teeth as the snow whitened his cap. "For now, I won't pull this trigger. But when we get inside there…I don't care where you're from, who you fought for or *what* the damned hell you are…you're gonna tell everybody straight what you know to be true 'bout this. Are you hearin' *me*?"

"I am. Now do what I'm telling you."

Rooster peered down the embankment again. Once more Lawson thought the young man was going to try to go after Tabbers, but then the rifle's barrel left Lawson's throat and Rooster followed Gantt and his lantern back toward the locomotive and the passenger car.

The vampire gunfighter stood alone.

But he was not alone for very long.

He sensed rather than saw the movement behind him, and in a blur he whirled around with the Colt full of silver angels ready to fire.

"You don't want to do that," said the little boy who sat atop the biggest boulder.

Seven.

THE BOY WAS MAYBE TWELVE years old, but Lawson knew that was only in appearance. He had been taken and turned young, that was for sure. The boy wore a white shirt with a ruffled collar and ruffles down the front; at least it had been white once, before it had become matted with dried blood. He wore gray short pants and cream-colored leggings, with old-fashioned buckled shoes. Above the pallid and grinning face the mass of curly, touselled hair was straw-colored, and the boy's eyes were light. Except now they held centers of crimson, and they were aimed at Trevor Lawson with not only malicious intent but a touch of true merriment. The boy was thin and awkward-looking; he had not been given time to fill out his bones.

"Hello," he said, in his high-pitched, childish voice. "I'm Henry."

Lawson nodded. His gun was ready. "I imagine you know my name."

"I do. We all do. Let me introduce myself a little better. I am...*was*...Henry Styles, Junior. You can call me Junior, if it pleases you."

"Nothing pleases me right now."

The little boy cackled and clapped his hands together. The fingernails were long, dirty claws that Lawson figured could rip the head from a human being in a matter of seconds.

When he was done laughing, Henry Styles Junior said, "Do you know how many there are of us out here?"

"Many," was Lawson's answer.

"We—*I*," he corrected, "brought an army. After what you did to LaRouge and the others at Nocturne...I kinda figured we needed to be more careful." The grin widened, so much that the fangs almost slid out. "I always liked the snow," he said. "Makes me think of Christmas in Philadelphia."

"Oh? That's where you're from?"

"Born in Philadelphia in the year..." Junior paused. "What year is this?"

"1886."

"Hm. Born in Philadelphia in the year 1781. That makes me—"

"Older than you look."

"*Smarter* than I look, too," Junior said. "They say you're smart too, Mr. Lawson."

"Nice of them to say."

"Are they correct?"

"I'd like to think so." While he was speaking, Lawson was scanning his surroundings; at any second he expected some monstrosity—similar to the shape-changing vampire he'd faced on a rooftop in New Orleans last summer—to attack from any direction.

"Ease yourself," said Junior. "We want to be gracious."

"Grace from one of *you*? I doubt you understand that concept."

The thing that looked like a boy laughed. A black tongue that might have been forked slid out from the mouth and caught some snowflakes before it withdrew.

"Your situation," the creature said, "is hopeless. You do realize that."

Lawson was about to deny it, but in truth he could not...at least not yet.

"And there you are. The truth of the matter. Let me tell you what we desire: yourself and Ann Kingsley. When you give yourselves up to us, we'll clear the track. The others can go on to wherever they're going, and long life to them."

"Does that include the man who's lying down in that brush? Or have you already drained him and torn him up?"

"Tut, tut," Junior said, with the fixed grin upon his warped mouth. "Sacrifices must be made, for the good of the many. I believe I recall President Washington saying such a thing."

"He's dead."

"Regrettably so. I wish we'd gotten to him first. What a leader he would've made for us!"

"I doubt that LaRouge would like to share the honor. Is she here?"

"As much as you would like her to be…no. She is at a distance, but you can be sure she's with us, in her own way."

It was disconcerting to Lawson, talking this way to a creature who looked like a little boy, spoke like an older man and thought like a monster. He had to get away, calm himself, and try to reason things through.

"Our terms," said Junior. "Give yourself and your lady friend up, or we take everyone. We'll take you and Miss Ann anyway, but I know you'll bring some of my tribe to harm and I dislike that certainty." He swung his legs back and forth on the boulder as any rambunctious tyke might, who didn't mind the wind temperature in the single digits. "We won't wait very long, Trevor. So for the sake of your newfound—"

"You won't have to wait at all," Lawson said, but even as he was squeezing the trigger to send a silver bullet through Junior's skull the creature whirled away so fast it was a white blur…then only empty space and a ripple in the snow where the body had been. Lawson had never seen one of them move so quickly as that, and he was both shocked and in awe of Junior's speed; so much so that his finger had not had time to depress the Colt's trigger to its firing point.

And then when Lawson turned away the thing that was crouched on top of the locomotive behind him sprang into the air, and from the rags of its shirt two ebony wings that had been folded in wait now exploded into their span of ten feet width.

The thing resembled a human being only for its having two legs, two arms, a torso and a head in addition to the wings; everything else was, as Easterly had said, an abomination. It was dark-fleshed and muscular and gnarled and greedy, and as it swooped in silence down from its perch upon Trevor Lawson the mouth gaped wide open to ready the curved fangs. Above it the eyes with their crimson pupils were hypnotically horrific, and the claws at the ends of the long fingers twitched in anticipation.

It came at him so fast that, again, Lawson was stunned and mostly for the fact that he had let himself be beguiled by Junior as this shapechanged vampire had crouched atop the engine. His Colt fired with a sharp *crack* but his aim was off. The bullet streaked past the thing's left side and continued on into the night like a small blue-flamed meteor. Lawson's own fangs slid out. He threw up his free arm to protect his face and throat. The claws reached for him and were only inches away, but the desire to survive sped Lawson's actions.

And also steadied his aim.

The second shot took the thing in the head, just above the left eye.

It was upon him before the sanctified bullet could take effect. It bore him to the ground. Lawson put his hand against the thing's chin to keep those fangs away. The claws dug into the shoulders of his coat and the bat-like wings fought the air.

In what seemed an agonizing length of time but was only a matter of seconds the creature shuddered and writhed and began to crack apart beginning at the hole above the left eye. Within the cracks a pulsing red heat glowed, as if the power of the consecrated silver was attacking the vampire's ichor. The misshapen face criss-crossed with cracks like that of a dried-up mummy. The thing tried to pull away from Lawson, as if getting back into the turbulent air would save it. Lawson did his best to hold onto it but it tore away from him with a strangled scream. Its eyes imploded, the left and then the right, even as the wings powered the body upward with the last of their massive strength. The face collapsed upon itself, the mouth caved in, the arms and legs flailed as more seething red fissures opened in the body.

Another pistol cracked. A large piece of the vampire's head with black hair attached to it blew out and burst into flame in midair. This second silver bullet sped the process of destruction, and even as Ann bent over Lawson to help him to his feet the creature was torn apart by the wind. The last to be dissolved were the wings, which fell into the snow in patterns of ash. What remained were the rags of the shirt, a pair of gray trousers and a pair of ordinary brown boots.

Lawson struggled up. Did he still have his hat? Yes, the leather chinstrap had held. His Colt? Yes, in his hand. Two bullets fired. Three, with Ann's. A pair of silvers wasted. He was dazed and for a terrible moment had been back in time on the battlefield at Shiloh, crawling away in desperate terror from the nightmarish army that grinned and capered with glee as they pursued him across a landscape of the dead.

"Get inside," he told her. "*Hurry*!"

"I heard the shots. I knew—"

"Come on!" he said, pulling her. There was no time. They were everywhere. A dark shape streaked through the air ten or twelve feet above their heads. The embankment to the right was coming alive with figures that appeared from the cover of trees, shrubs and rocks. On the left side, where the cliffs rose up, more figures seemed to be emerging from the very stones. As Lawson pulled Ann with him, his gaze fell upon one of the dead shapechanger's boots lying in the ashen snow.

It held a spur.

"*Move*!" he said, aware that on both sides the earth was vomiting forth a hideous horde. They had reached the engine when a single voice cried out through the wind.

It said, *"Ann! Annie! Wait for me, Annie!"*

She caught her breath and might have fallen had Lawson not been holding her.

"Trevor!" she said, as the tears streaked down her cheeks. "It's my father!"

"No, it's not."

"They have him! Listen to him! He's still alive!"

"Annie! Please...don't leave me...!"

"Let's go!" He was prepared to pick her up if she resisted but she did not, though her knees had weakened and she staggered the rest of the way to the passenger car.

Ann had left Rooster with his rifle and Eric with his pistol in charge of keeping everyone where they needed to be. When she and Lawson came into the car, Reverend Easterly was on his knees beside Blue, who had regained consciousness and was holding his hand. Eric stood over him, his pistol drawn but held down at his side. Gantt was sitting toward the front, the lantern on the seat beside him, his face seamed with worry. The others were still sitting where they'd been when Ann had left the car. Rooster's rifle swung toward the door.

The fireman said, "Put that gun away and get to talkin'!"

Lawson ignored him. He holstered his Colt and shut the door, then he helped Ann to a seat and went back to see about Blue.

"Did you *hear* me, Alabama?" Rooster had shouted it; his patience had shredded with the sound of the shots. "Who were you shootin' at out there?"

"Not who," Ann managed to say, her voice listless. She slid her revolver into its holster. "*What*."

As Lawson approached, Easterly started to stand up and retreat but instead he corrected himself. He remained where he was, his hand still grasping the girl's. Blue's eyes had opened, though they were still nearly swollen shut with pain. "Where am I?" she whispered. "Where am I?"

"I've told you," Easterly said gently, "you're on a train. You're being taken to Helena, to the hospital there."

"A t...train?"

"Yes."

There was a pause. Blue tried to lift her head, but it was too much effort for her.

"Where am I?" she whispered. And then, "Ohhhhh... I'm h...hurtin'." The swollen eyes searched, and what they could see or not see was anyone's guess. "Am…I… dy…dy…" She gave it up, for again it was taking too much precious strength.

"Have faith," said Easterly, in as soft as voice as Lawson had ever heard a man speak. "We're going to get you to that hospital. Aren't we, Mr. Lawson?" His heavy-lidded eyes moved up upon the vampire.

"That's the plan."

Blue shivered. "C…c…cold," she whispered, though the blanket was still around her and the passenger car was so sturdily built as to let only a few small shrills of wind in. She began to cough…once…twice…a third time more violently even as Easterly tried to calm her. A little thread of blood ran from the corner of her mouth, and Lawson found himself staring at the vein that gave a weak pulse at her throat.

Her coughing subsided, but her breathing had become harsh. Lawson took from his coat the small bottle that Fossie had given him, and was grateful his clash with the winged monster hadn't smashed it. "The doctor gave me this for her," he said as he offered it to Easterly. "It's morphine and whisky, to help her sleep."

"I think," said the reverend, "that she'll be sleeping well enough very soon, don't you?"

"Give her a sip if she needs it." Lawson could do nothing more for the girl. It looked as if Fossie's Mule Punch wouldn't be necessary for the moment, because

Blue's eyes had closed and she had—thankfully—drifted off again. "Watch her carefully, will you?"

Easterly nodded, and Lawson could tell he was sincere in his regard for the girl's life. He figured it was probably because Easterly had stolen so many men from their wives and children in his past life as a back-shooting bounty hunter. Lawson turned away to give his attention to Rooster, who had come along the aisle with his rifle ready and his face contorted in a snarl of anger and fear.

"Who you shootin' at?" Rooster demanded. "How come you lettin' Mr. Tabberson lie out there and die? Come on, *tell us*!"

"Watch that gun, Rooster," Gantt cautioned, though his voice was weak.

"Pardon, Mr. Gantt sir, but hush up! I'm wantin' to know what Alabama's got us into! That fella says he's a warbuck, I'm kinda believin' it's so!"

"That's what I think!" Mathias had stood up from his seat. "You should've seen him back at the Palace! And look at him now! There's something mighty wrong about this gent!"

"I am not a warlock," said Lawson, and he spoke it loudly and forcefully enough to silence all other voices.

"What I am," he went on, into the small noise of the wind keening around the car, "is a vampire." He moved his gaze from face to face and found them all frozen. "Well...a correction. I'm not entirely gone...that is, not entirely like one of the things that has blocked this track and has taken Mr. Tabberson to his death…or worse. They're out there in a large number. If they got in here or got to you out there, they would either take you to be turned or they would drink you dry and then tear you apart. I could do that too, if I were of a mind."

"Wait a minute, wait a damned chicken-pickin' minute!" Rebinaux said, and he too was on his feet. "What the hell is a *vampire*? I thought you said you was from Alabama!"

Lawson grunted. This was going to take a little demonstration.

"Mathias," he said, "do you have a coin?"

"Yeah, *why*?"

"Take the coin and throw it as hard as you can against the front wall."

"Huh?"

"Just do it. As hard as you can."

Mathias removed from his trouser pocket a small coin. He shook his head as if he thought Lawson utterly insane, and then he reared his arm back and threw the coin with all his strength a distance of a little more than twelve feet.

"Pitching is not your game," said Lawson, as he leaned against the front wall next to the door. He opened his right fist to show in his palm the Liberty Seated ten-cent piece.

They had not seen him move. He had been standing several feet behind Mathias one instant, and in the next he was at the far wall, waiting there at his leisure. He had gone along the aisle past Rooster and the Winchester hardly leaving a swirl of disturbed air. Rooster's back was still to him when Lawson spoke, and when he spun around he brought the rifle's barrel up again aimed at the other man's chest.

"Easy, Ann," he said, because she'd drawn her gun once more and it was levelled at Rooster's head. "It's not me you have to fear," he told the group. "It's those things out there. Lead bullets can hurt me, but they can't kill me or my kind. There are two ways to do that: a consecrated silver bullet through the skull, or cutting the head off. I'm sure you have questions, but be brief. We have to figure out a plan of—"

"A *vampire,*" said Reverend Easterly. He had risen to his feet from Blue's side. "I'm not an uneducated man. I've even read Polidori's book. I would say you are a lunatic, sir, but I'm afraid I know better."

"Good. That advances us somewhat."

"Of all the Satan-spawned garbage on this earth and in the world beyond...I never thought I'd see the likes of *you*. I've heard of your kind for years, but to *see* one..." Easterly had the crucifix between his hands again and held onto it as if to dear life itself. "They have been the subject of legends in Europe for hundreds of years," he told the others, but his eyes never left Lawson. "Spawn of the Devil, the very worst disciples of evil under the sun."

"Under the moon, to be exact," said Lawson.

"I thought them fiction," the reverend went on. "A figment of a mad imagination. But now...seeing you... *knowing* you. Why don't you tell them what you drink to give yourself a so-called eternal life?"

"I'll do better. I'll show them." He decided to put on a display of his speed again, and within an eyeblink he had passed Rooster once more and was opening the large canvas bag that Ann had brought aboard holding his clothes, his protective black shroud, and other items. From the bag he took another of the Japanese bottles. He uncorked it, held it over his open mouth and poured. The blood ran out onto his tongue, which fortunately had not yet become forked nor turned black but it *was* the color of gray ash. He closed his mouth and felt the blood being absorbed by the hollow fangs in their pits in his upper jaw. It was a delicious taste, though it had somewhat of a stockyard flavor; nothing could come close nor was nearly as satisfying or as strength-giving as the real thing.

Lawson corked the bottle again and said with gore on his lips, "Cattle blood, gentlemen. A priest friend of mine in New Orleans secures it for me. What Reverend Easterly is trying to tell you is that vampires drink human blood. And yes, this is true." He dropped the bottle back into the bag with a smile.

Then he propelled himself at Eli Easterly. His smile was gone.

Human eyes could not follow him at his half-speed; the human mind could not comprehend his full speed. He was there and then he was not, as if he'd abruptly vanished. In the next heartbeat he was in Easterly's terror-stricken face, and the terror was intensified when Lawson's mouth opened wide, the lower jaw unhinged and from the upper jaw the fangs slid out. Easterly's crucifix came up; with no effort Lawson knocked the man's hand aside and the Cross flew away across the car.

Lawson grasped the man's collar and spun him around, standing behind him to face the rifle Rooster held and—yes—the pistol the soul-shaken Eric aimed at him too.

"Lisssssten to me, every one of you!" he said, as he allowed the fangs to retract and his mouth to properly arrange itself. "You can think of me as a monster, that's fine. There's a war going on, and Ann and I are in it. You are too. I'm sorry for that but it can't be helped. Now...together, we've got to figure a way out of this. We could try to wait them out, until sunrise, but they won't allow that. You're going to have to follow my directions or before this night is over you'll either be dead or you'll be on the way to being turned...which will make you like them. Or *me*. And gentlemen, just *look* at what I am. You have *no* damned idea what this is like. I am a dead man walking...but by God I won't be destroyed by *them*. Or taken by them, and I'll protect Ann and all of you as best I can." He looked from face to face. It might have been a trick of the lamplight, but everyone seemed to have gone a few shades gray. Even Rooster.

"Any questions?" Lawson asked.

The wind shrieked and the snow was blown in white gusts past the windows. Otherwise there was silence.

Then: "They must want something. What is it they want?"

"They want me," Lawson said to Mathias. He released Easterly, who to his credit did not cringe nor fall to his knees in terror, but simply lowered his head and went over to retrieve his crucifix. "And they want Ann. I spoke to one out there who I think is their leader. He looks like a twelve-year-boy but he's far from it. He said if Ann and I give ourselves up, they'll let all of you go."

"Well...*hell*..." said Rebinaux, but he sounded as if his mouth was stuffed with cotton bolls.

"If you want to save us," said Presco, who was near jabbering, "then...that's the only way, ain't it? Lord Jesus and Holy Joe, I don't want to be et up or turned into no blood-sucker!"

"Unfortunately," Lawson answered, "they *lie*. As soon as they had us, there would be nothing to stop them from going through this car like a roomful of flying knives. And if you think you could get outside and outrun them…I'm twenty-five years turned, gents. Some of them will be eighty…ninety…a hundred years or more. They get faster with age."

"Shit creek," Gantt muttered. His eyes were wild. "We're up shit creek, ain't we? I mean…I can't hardly believe what I'm—"

The conductor was interrupted when something came out of the woods on the right.

It slammed against the window between Mathias and Eric with a force that nearly shattered the glass. Even so, the window cracked with a gunshot noise along the diagonal. Stuck there for a few seconds was a bloody mass that had an eyeless face and a flame-red beard. The mouth was open, but there was nothing inside the mouth but the darkness of the night beyond.

The naked skin of Jack Tabberson slid down the glass, leaving thick scrawls of gore to mark its slow passage. Then it fell away, into the snow.

Eight.

KEENE PRESCO BEGAN TO LAUGH.

It began almost as a low stutter, then it went high and wild, and the bearded bear of a man staggered and almost fell and suddenly in his laugh there was a choking sound that might have been the birth of a cry of terror.

"Hold on to yourself!" To Lawson's surprise, it was the reverend who'd spoken the command. Easterly's voice rang out so forcefully that it stopped Presco's cry in mid-choke. "There's no use in that!" Easterly continued. All eyes were upon him. "Whatever this...*man* is," he said, motioning toward Lawson, "we've got to trust him." His face betrayed the disgust he felt at saying that. "Before God I never imagined such a company as this, but here we are."

"I've got this rifle!" Rooster said. He had turned his back on the bloody window. "I'll take 'em down bullet by bullet!"

"Like I told you, lead can hurt them but it can't kill," said Lawson. "Ann, how many silvers do you have?"

She checked her holster, counting with her fingers. She had one silver to every three leads. "Five in the cylinder, eight in the holster. Twenty more in my bag." She took the opportunity to slide a sixth silver into the pistol.

"Good. I've got thirty, plus the four in my gun and two in the derringer."

"How many would you say are out there?"

"I couldn't tell." Lawson balked at saying *Very many*, because the truth would only further fray raw nerves. He didn't want anyone panicking and trying to run for their lives through the snow...they'd end up like Tabberson, if the vampires were in a mood to be merciful. He saw in her face that she wanted to ask another question... *My father, among them*? He looked away, and on this subject Ann did not pursue him.

"This ain't *happenin'*!" Rebinaux's voice was as choked as Presco's had been. "Man alive, I'm sittin' in the Palace drunker'n eight skunks! This just ain't—"

There came the sound of someone walking on the front platform.

The door's glass inset was dirty with coal smoke, but through it could be seen the top of a small boy's head, the wind-touselled hair, and the blurred upper portion of the pallid face. A hand rose up, became a fist, and knocked at the glass.

"That's the boy?" Mathias asked. He had gotten himself under control and was eerily calm, as if at the bottom of his barrel had been a courage that he'd not expected to find.

"He calls himself Junior," Lawson answered. "And remember, he's not a boy."

"Boy, warbuck or blood-sucker," said Rooster, "I'll put a slug right 'twixt his eyes!"

"Steady." Lawson took two strides toward him, reached out and grasped the rifle's barrel. He pushed it toward the ceiling. "All you're going to do is make him *mad*." The fist knocked again on the glass, with insistence. With no effort Junior could shatter that glass and let the wind in to gnaw at everyone whose veins carried human blood. "Let's find out a little more about him and our situation."

"Our *situation*? We're at the damned gates of *Hell*, ain't we?" Gantt asked.

"Everyone be easy," Lawson cautioned. He approached the door. "Rooster, take your finger off that trigger. Eric, put your gun down." The young Cavanaugh failed to respond. "*Eric*!" Lawson said, in a sharper tone, and this time he was obeyed.

Lawson opened the door. The wind and snow blew in past Henry Styles Junior, who smiled up at his opponent with boy-sized teeth that had a space between the front two.

"Are you free to talk?" Junior asked.

"I am."

"A fine assortment here." The creature had quickly taken appraisal of the passengers, as if he'd just opened a box of candies. His gaze snagged on the wounded girl. His chin lifted and his nostrils flared. "*Oh*," he said, "she smells delicious. But she's dying, isn't she?"

"I've heard what you want. Is there anything else?"

"Yes indeed." He came in and closed the door behind him, but he ventured no further into the car. He locked eyes for a few seconds with Eli Easterly before he returned his full attention to Lawson. "We don't want these blood-puppets. We want you and Miss Kingsley. They'll be free to go, as soon as you disarm yourselves and we have you. You know, her father wishes to see her. Would you like that?" He offered Ann a ghastly smile, but she made no reply.

"And your sister too," Junior went on. "Eva's here. Yes, that's right. This will be a family reunion." When Ann still gave no response, Junior's gaze shifted to Lawson. "What point is there to resist, Trevor? You're searching for LaRouge; she wants to see *you*. All will be taken care of, all will be as it should be. But...Trevor, let these humans go on their way, won't you? And that girl there...shouldn't she be getting to a doctor?"

"We both know that you won't let this train pass," said Lawson. "*Granting* life is not in your nature. I *know,* Henry...because part of me is what *you* are. Didn't you ever want to fight it? Didn't you—"

"It is a losing battle," came the answer, in the voice of a little boy grown cold over the span of decades. "A foolish endeavor, leading to extermination. Miss Kingsley?" he called. "Would you like to see your father and sister now?"

"My father and sister," she managed to say, "are dead."

"You have that wrong...Ann, if I may. What they have found—and all of us have found—is true life. A life of abundance and *power* beyond the dreams of blood puppets and their faulty beliefs." He fired a quick scornful glance at Easterly. "What you think of as life is *death,* Ann. Look at your friend Lawson here. He knows it's true, because part of him wants to take hold of this life, to revel in it, to experience the fullness of our rapture, to never perish. Don't let him lie to you and say he does not. And here he is now, making his *stand.*" Junior grinned; it was not a pretty sight. His eyes glinted red and his lower jaw appeared misshapen, as if near jumping out of joint. Lawson figured the blood smell of Tabberson had fired them all up into a frenzy, and now this aroma of Blue's blood was working on him in the close confines of the car.

"Making his *pointless* stand," Junior said, "and dooming all of you fine people to a tortured fate." The child-vampire swept his arm across in a motion that seemed to be pulling his audience into his chest. "Well, he's just plain *selfish*! What your engineer got was a quick release. Yours will be a long experience." His smile, like a jagged razor slash, centered upon Lawson. "Ten minutes, sir. That is your...shall we say...deadline."

"Here's your damn deadline," said Rooster, and fired his rifle from the hip.

The blast made an explosive sound within the car. A bullet hole appeared in the wall behind Junior, along with a splatter of thick black ichor. The Winchester slug had passed through his body on the left side.

Junior rocked back on his heels, then righted himself. His smile had faded only a fraction. He touched his shirt where the black stain was spreading. Lawson knew that the ichor would stop flowing within a few seconds, sealing the wound at both entrance and exit. Already the ichor would be healing any damage to the mysterious dead-in-life internals of the vampire. Lawson knew; he himself felt as if he were withering from the inside out.

"I think that broke a rib or two," Junior said. "Ohhhhh...you will *so* regret—"

Ann's gun had come up. Her face was a study of cold fury. She pulled the trigger.

Henry Styles Junior for all of his one hundred and five years was the quickest vampire Lawson had ever seen. Even as Ann's pistol cracked and the silver angel blasted from its barrel, Junior had hurled himself headlong at the window to his right. He was smashing through the glass as the consecrated slug passed his blurred shape and smacked into the wall. Then he was gone, leaving the wind to blow snow through the broken window and small bits of glass to fall with the sound of tinkling chimes.

At once Lawson was at the window with his vampire-killing Colt drawn. He scanned the night, seeing rocks and wind-twisted trees but no trace of movement from the Dark Society.

"That was not very smart," he said to Rooster, and he did not fail to note that the rifle was now aimed at his own midsection. "Please, let's not be *really* foolish."

"Hell, what do you expect?" Rebinaux's voice had gone as high as a flute. "We just gonna sit and wait here to get killed? I'm for runnin' for it! Get my ass outta here while I can! Deuce...Keene...you with me?"

"Yeah," said Presco. "I'm with you. I ain't stayin' here and waitin' to be et!" He gave a brief glance at Ann's pistol. "You can shoot me if you please, but I'm gettin'! Deuce, how about it?"

Mathias was a few seconds in answering. "You won't make it fifty feet from this train. Look what they did to that engineer." He shivered. "Can somebody draw the curtain on that window? It's going to get real cold in here, real—"

Quick, he was about to say, but it came more quickly than he'd thought.

A SHOT RANG out. The bullet broke through the next window and knocked a chunk from the seatback in front of Eric. A second and third bullets finished the job on that window. More gunfire erupted from the other side of the train. "Get down!" Lawson shouted, as the glass began to be shattered from every window along the car. A slug shrieked past Lawson's head and broke the glass behind him. One of the oil lamps was hit and spilled its burning fuel upon the floorboards. As Ann dove for the floor to cover Blue, a bullet ricocheting off the edge of a window clipped the brim of her cap and knocked it off her head. Gantt cried out in pain as wood splinters pierced the side of his face. Mathias felt a bullet pass so close to his skull he thought it might have left a part in his hair. Rooster was firing back, standing in the aisle shooting from one side to another and seemingly oblivious to being hit though the slugs were zipping by him to the left and the right. "Get down!" Lawson hollered at him, and at last the fireman seemed to realize the danger he was in. One last shot into the night and he threw himself down between two seats just as a couple of hornets passed through where he'd been standing.

The barrage of bullets went on for maybe fifteen more seconds. When it ended every window had been opened to the bitter cold and the walls of the passenger car had been pierced by at least twenty slugs.

In the aftermath of the gunshots there was the noise of the wind shrieking through the splintered frames and the crackling of the fire gnawing at the floorboards. Lawson crawled to the puddle of burning oil, took his coat off and mashed the flames down. It occurred to him that in short order the freezing temperatures would make the humans long for the warmth of a fire, but for now they couldn't be forced out into the open any more than they already were.

"Jesus! Jesus!" Rebinaux was saying, from his huddled position on the floor.

Lawson could smell fresh blood; someone had taken a slug. "Who's hit?"

"Took a faceful of splinters," Gantt croaked. "Damn close."

"I'm all right," Ann said. "Lost my cap."

"The girl?"

"She wasn't hit."

"Anyone else? Eric?"

"I'm okay."

"Easterly?"

"Untouched," he answered.

"I'm good," said Rooster.

"Mathias?" Lawson prodded.

"All right...for the moment."

"Lord...God...I'm hit," said the rusty sawblade voice of Keene Presco. "Busted my damn collarbone... left side."

"How bad?"

"Hurts somethin' awful...bleedin'...but I don't think I'm dyin'." Another shot was fired into the passenger car, followed by a second and a third, but there were no cries of pain or panic. Lawson figured the bullets had come in one glassless window and out one opposite. *Wanting us to keep our heads down,* he thought. *Particularly* my *head and Ann's.* He took a moment to dump the lead from his second Colt and arm it with the silvers.

"Alabama?" Rooster called from further along the car. "You got any ideas?"

"Keeping from being shot is the first one."

"If you're like that *thing,*" said Mathias, "you don't have much to worry about."

"It would be an inconvenience I'd rather not endure."

"You gotta get us outta this!" Rebinaux piped up. "You and me, we're brothers from Dixie, ain't we? You can't let *me* die!"

Lawson didn't know how to answer that, so he remained silent.

"Gettin' mighty cold in here," Gantt said.

And then, from outside, a voice called that at first seemed to be part of the wind.

"Annie?" it said. *"Annie, come to a window!"*

Lawson heard her make a choking sound that wrenched at his heart.

"Annie? Eva's here with me! Eva's here!"

"You *know* one of those monsters?" Easterly asked.

"Her father and sister," Lawson said, so Ann wouldn't have to. "Both taken and turned."

"Annie? Baby? Look out here at us!"

"You know what they mean to do," said the vampire.

"Shoot me in the head as soon as I raise up. They've likely got a rifle already aimed."

"Ann? Sssspeak to me, ssssister!"

That voice was the worst; it was at once both a fierce demand and a pitiful entreaty, and Lawson knew it must be repulsing Ann and pulling at her in equal measures. She had not seen her father or sister in months; did she dare now to lift her head over the bullet-riddled sill to lay eyes upon what her family had become?

"I love you, Ann! I sssstill love you!"

"I've got the direction fixed," Ann said quietly, but enough to reach Lawson. "Standing about eight feet apart, maybe twenty…twenty-five feet from the window next to me."

"Come to us, Annie! We can all be together again!"

"Lawson?" Ann called.

"Yes?"

"I can do it."

"I know you can," he said. "Do you want me to—"

"No."

He heard the hammer of her pistol being cocked, even though she was muffling the noise under her coat.

From where he crouched on the floor he couldn't see her toward the rear of the car, but he knew she was readying herself for what she needed to do. He started to say *Careful* but he did not, for he knew she would be... and this she had to do alone.

"*We're waiting for you, Ann,*" Eva called. "*Come join ussss...join ussss.*" The eerie voice was whipped away by the wind.

Ann had to strike while she could still locate them by sound.

She lifted her head.

Through the falling snow she saw their shapes, standing about eight feet apart but maybe thirty feet away instead of twenty; the wind had done that trickery. She had the impression of ragged figures, like a pair of impoverished beggars. She could make out no facial features and she didn't want to. All she could tell was that one was taller than the other though they both were sickeningly thin. She brought her gun up and took a fraction of a second to eyeball where she wanted the silver slug to go.

Her finger was on the trigger. Already the creature who had once been Eva Kingsley was whirling away, long dark hair flying in the wind, but the shade of David Kingsley had stepped forward, both arms outstretched toward her.

"*My Annie,*" he said, and he sounded to be in terrible pain.

She caught a glimpse of the gore that covered the front of his shirt and his suit coat. She dared not look into his face. She heard the high report of a rifle being fired from amid the rocks to her left. Without flinching she fired her revolver at the same instant as the bullet hit the windowframe beside her.

She didn't have to wait to know that the bullet had struck the center of his forehead. When the second rifle bullet passed through where her own head had been, Ann was crouched down on the floorboards with the smoking gun pressed to her bosom and her eyes squeezed tightly shut.

Lawson lifted his head and saw the figure burning, breaking apart in red-rimmed fissures, turning to ashes that would be scattered upon the rocks and through the trees of this wild country, a long way from the boardrooms and banks of Louisiana.

The creature that had been David Kingsley perished in silence, but just before his head imploded he looked up into the snowfall though by then he had no eyes.

As he crumbled and the empty clothes fell, there came from the distance a feminine scream that started off as a cry of despair and became a shriek of rage. Lawson at the moment was thankful he couldn't see Ann's face.

Something hit the top of the car. Then came the sound of another weight, following seconds after.

"What's that?" Gantt directed the question to Lawson, but in truth he knew what it must be. And he answered it himself: "One of 'em's up there!"

"Two," said Lawson. He was already bracing for what had to be coming next.

A tremendous blow was struck to the roof of the car; the entire car trembled and the boards whined in protest. Another blow was struck…a third, and a fourth, two of the winged shapechangers at work, tearing off the lid of this box to get at the sweetmeats within. The things sounded as if they were using iron hammers, but Lawson figured they only needed their fists and claws.

Rooster dug into his coat, brought out more shells for his rifle and reloaded. He started to stand up. Lawson said, "They're waiting for that," and Rooster settled to the floor again.

A third weight landed atop the car. They were near breaking through. The roof was cracking, the boards bending inward. Rooster fired upward…two shots, but the creatures didn't slow their assault.

"All right," Lawson said, mostly to himself, because he figured he had about twenty seconds before the things got in. He was up and out the door at the back of the car before Ann or any of the others had fully registered that he'd moved, and so fast that even the vampires hiding amid the rocks with guns were unable to mark him as a target. Outside, he swung upon the metal ladder that gave access to the roof and jumped the rest of the way.

The three winged horrors that were beating the roof to pieces turned toward him as one when his boots hit the surface. There were two males and a female, all of them gray-fleshed and sinewy, dressed in rags, the female with long silver hair and one of the males missing his left arm at the elbow. Lawson had time to think that this male might have been stolen from a battlefield just as he had been, and then he shot the creature between the eyes and the thing screamed as it burned. It fell away, its skull crisscrossed with red fissures, its wings beating holes in the flurry of snow.

Then the other two were upon him.

The female was the faster of the two. She was leaping at him before he could get his Colt trained on her. At the same time, gunshots rang out from the rocks to his left and from the woods to his right. Bullets zipped past as Lawson fought the female's claws from getting at his eyes. The male swooped at him. Lawson shoved the female away. She went off the top of the car but her claws took most of his waistcoat with her. Along with it went his derringer in its inner pocket. A bullet tore into his right arm just above the elbow, paralyzing his gunhand. He drew his second Colt with his left hand, dodged a claw aimed at his face, felt the stinging pain of a second bullet grazing the back of his neck, and fired into the male creature's skull.

As the vampire convulsed and burned before him, Lawson was struck in the right side by another bullet. He knew fear. It came to him that this could be the end of the line for both himself and Ann. For all his quickness and power there were too many of them. He could see more of the winged shapechangers coming at him from the woods and the rocks. How they achieved this ability he didn't know, but at the moment he was sure he didn't have it.

More shots were fired. Ann, Rooster and Eric were firing from the car. The female vampire came at him once more, with renewed determination. Her claws grasped his shoulders and her fangs yearned toward his throat. She had nearly snapped shut on him when he put the Colt's barrel under her chin and fired a shot that sent the bullet through the top of her head. Still she held onto him as she began to break apart, and even as her eyeballs sank in and her gaping mouth became a hole in which the fangs melted like candle wax her claws dug deep and her wings were beating, trying to lift him off the roof.

She got him up about six feet in the air before her skull sizzled away, her arms fell from the rags of her body and the wings collapsed like burning black paper.

Lawson got off a shot at the creature coming at him from the right but the thing dodged aside in midair and the bullet streaked on over the trees. The female vampire's hands, both aflame, were still clenched to his shoulders and when he shook them off they flew away in ashes.

There were too many, and too many bullets being fired at him. He holstered his gun and as he scrabbled down the ladder a slug ricocheted off the metal. He got back into the car, slammed the door shut and threw himself onto his belly, where he crawled like a wounded animal between two seats and lay there leaking ichor that smelled of a sulphur pit in Hell.

Nine.

"HOW MANY DID YOU TAKE?" Ann was leaning over him. The firing had stopped and for the moment there was just the high sharp cry of the wind.

"A couple." Lawson winced and touched his hurt side with his left hand. The ichor had turned that part of his shirt ebony, as well as his right sleeve. "Damn it," he said. The pain was more nagging than severe. His damage would heal in a few hours, though he'd be slowed down until everything had knitted together again. That was part of their aim in shooting him; not to kill, because that was impossible with the plain lead slugs, but to steal his speed and resolve. "I won't be able to use my right hand for awhile. My arm's broken." He reached back and put his fingers against the hot line a bullet had grazed across the nape of his neck. "Lucky there. I wouldn't like to know what a broken neck feels like."

"*Trevor.*" She had spoken his name in nearly a whisper, and though her face was still composed it was a mask, because Lawson saw in her eyes that she was fighting the same fear that had hit him up on the car's roof. "What are we going to *do*?"

"We won't give up," he said, in answer to what she was really asking.

"Those things have got us trapped!" It was Gantt's voice from further up front. He sounded at his breaking point. "Lawson! This is your fight, not ours! Listen...listen...all of you...do we deserve to be slaughtered? What have we done to get into this?"

"Steady up, Mister Gantt," said Rooster.

"*Steady up*? Do you *want* to die?"

"No...ain't what none of us want."

"It's *his* fight, Rooster! We don't have no damned part in this!"

"Sir...that's where you're wrong."

The voice that had spoken those five words surprised Lawson; it belonged to Eli Easterly. The reverend had remained near Blue. The girl was semiconscious. Easterly had been at her side to console her and also to keep her calm if she came more fully awake. Snow had blown in and whitened the man's hair and eyebrows, which along with his gray-toned flesh and gaunt features made him appear more vampiric than even Lawson.

"Whatsay?" Gantt fired back.

"You are wrong," Easterly repeated. "It is our fight, too."

"Hell it is!" Rebinaux squawked. "I ain't done nothin' to them things!"

"You don't have to," said the reverend, as he placed a hand on Blue's forehead; her eyes had opened, and she was whispering that she was cold. He adjusted her blanket as best he could. "It seems to me that whatever Mr. Lawson is, he is by far not the worst of them. Before getting on this train I never would've thought such a thing possible...that I would feel I should *help* him survive in whatever way I can, instead of calling upon the Lord to destroy him and the rest of his tribe."

"Think again, preacher!" said Presco. "Your Lord ain't listenin'!"

"The Lord does listen, but He depends on the human hand to do the work. Or the hand of whatever is available. In this case, Mr. Lawson." He gave Blue as much of a smile as he could muster. "Shhhhh," he said. "Just rest...close your eyes...rest..."

"You're crazy! We cain't fight 'em! I ain't stayin' here waitin' to die, I'm gettin' out!" Presco stood up, his bloodied right hand pressed to the wound near his collarbone. "Somebody come with me!" he said, his eyes wild. "Johnny, let's you and me—"

The bullet came from the right side of the train, down amid the trees. It took off a chunk of Presco's jaw. As he turned toward the gunfire with an expression of righteous indignation, like a man who has brushed against a hornet's nest, the second bullet hit him in the upper chest and the third one, fired from the left side of the train, got him in the brainpan. He pitched forward with a small grunt, really a soft exhalation of breath, probably the softest sound the man had ever made in his life.

He slithered down amid the seats, twitched a few times and then was still.

There was a long moment of silence.

"Bloodsuckers with guns," said Mathias. He gave a hard, hollow laugh. "Kick my ass and call me Fannie."

"More than guns." Eric had dared to lift his head to peer out the window to the left, then he ducked down again. "Riders coming."

Both Lawson and Ann took a chance to look. Two riders were approaching on horses. Lawson recalled the spur he'd seen on the shapechanger's boot. He didn't like this; it smelled of something he'd never experienced before. The vampires riding on the horses had already transformed themselves into the winged creatures, but their wings were folded back along their sides. One looked to be wearing a cavalry's officer's cap. The horses showed no signs of being skittish with those things on their backs, and this is what made Lawson ask himself: *Could an animal be turned?*

The question was hanging there when the two riders spread their wings into the wind and left their saddles. The horses continued on through the snow, and as they neared the passenger car they began to change into beasts from a madman's nightmare.

Their flesh, leathery at the beginning, rippled and hardened like overlapping scales of thorny armor plate. Their heads lengthened and malformed into what Lawson thought might have resembled the ancient descriptions of dragons roaming the haunted forests of old Europe. One of the creatures began to grow two more legs from its sides that pushed it along more like a spider than a horse.

They were not slowing, but coming at full gallop and slither.

"Brace yourselves!" Lawson shouted.

The first smashed into the left side of the passenger car. The other hit a heartbeat after. The car's wall burst inward in a shower of broken planks, splinters and the rest of the glass from the windowframes. The entire car shuddered and nearly was torn off the rails and its couplings to the coal car ahead and the freight car behind. In the chaos of destruction Lawson saw that Easterly had thrown himself over Blue as protection and Ann had put an arm up to shield her own face from the flying debris.

Then the pair of shapechanged creatures began to thrash their way in, their flesh and heads more reptilian than equine. Below the red centers of their eyes their massive jaws opened to reveal the sliding forth of curved fangs the size of butcher knives.

Rooster had fallen back against the opposite side of the car. He had lost his rifle in the impact. Lawson heard Gantt gibbering with terror. Rebinaux had broken and was sobbing like a child, and he was trying desperately to crawl away from the monster whose head weaved back and forth above him, the jaws opened and the fangs glinting with light from burning pools of lamp fuel.

Lawson lifted his Colt to fire, but so stunned was he by these Hellish visions that his left trigger finger was too slow. Before he could get his shot off the creature's head darted down and the jaws engulfed Rebinaux's skull up to the throat. The thing's bite squeezed off the man's swelling scream; with a twist of its head it all but decapitated Johnny Rebinaux and then lifted the body off the planks as a man might lift a bottle to drink after its cork has been bitten out.

It was then that Lawson got his senses back and sent a bullet into the monster's head, but even as it twisted and writhed and began to break into burning pieces it backed out of the shattered car with Rebinaux's neck still clamped in its fangs, determined to feast on its final meal of human blood.

The second beast, the one that had become a nightmare combination of horse, spider and dragon, continued to push its way in. The fangs snapped at Rooster's legs. Ann got off a shot and hit the thing at the base of the neck. It gave a high shriek of pain and its head turned toward her, but then it was hit by three shots in quick succession in the meat of the body. The creature's head swivelled to go after Deuce Mathias, who stood amid the broken seats with the smoke of Rooster's Winchester swirling around him.

Lawson's and Ann's pistols fired nearly together. The two silvers pierced the thing's skull about three inches apart, and thus quickened its demise. As the thing cracked apart and its flesh sizzled like bacon in a skillet, it still focused on Mathias with its single remaining eyeball. When it lunged at him he held his ground and struck out, using the rifle as a club because the magazine was empty; the eyeball withered and sank in, the head began to collapse, and the wind whipped the body into a storm of ebony ashes.

A portion of the car's roof caved in. The two winged vampires that had ridden the horses in had hammered their way through. Ann shot the first one just below its cavalry cap as it dropped down into the car. In its death-throes it became a maddened whirlwind of fangs and claws. It ripped bloody wounds across Gantt's chest and then spun toward Eric, who shot the thing twice more at pointblank range just as the body collapsed like a punctured cyst and burned out of the dirty rags of its uniform.

The second vampire thought better of entering the car and took to the air. There came a few seconds during which the noise of the wind was nearly louder than Gantt's cursing as he lay with his back against a splintered wall, his hands pressed to his wounds.

Lawson saw them coming first, and then Ann. "Load up!" he told everyone who had a gun. "Here they come!"

The vampiric army of Henry Styles Junior was on the advance. They were not at full speed yet, but that was only a matter of seconds. There were maybe thirty of them on the left: men, women and what might be mistaken as children, some in blood-daubed rags but others well-dressed, as if they had come from the same world of humans that Lawson masqueraded in. Some had become nothing more than blood-hungry wild animals and those were the ones that rushed forward most greedily, while others with more decorum and restraint stayed at the rear. Or, Lawson figured, those were the vampires who had a steady supply of food and walked most freely among humans. He noted that those were also the ones who held the firearms. A few of the winged shapechangers perched on the rocks, crouched down as if settling in to enjoy the coming spectacle.

A check to the right showed fifteen or so more of Junior's army coming up the embankment through the snowy woods. They were in all manner of dress, again some ragged and bloodstained, others more freshly-procured: buckskins, fancy gowns, banker's suits, the patched clothing of dirt-poor farmers and their wives, little dresses and knickers for the things that had been turned as children.

Lawson had a thought that took hold of him as firmly as a vampire's claw.

They have come from all points of the Dark Society's compass. Directed and drawn here by LaRouge, because she wants me.

Me.

I could learn to be a god, he thought.

Of what use is the human world to me anymore? I am beyond it. I am strong and fast and if I pleased I could live forever. My wife and daughter...gone...a painful memory. I have been betrayed by the human kind, led to slaughter and abandonment at Shiloh. What do I owe them? Why should I hold onto that life...and...really...I am tired...so very tired...I cannot hold on.

If I give myself up, they may let Ann and the rest of them go. If I stop trying, they may yet live...

If...if...

A dangerous word.

"Do you want me to take this side or the other?"

He looked into Ann's eyes and he thought she flinched just a little, because perhaps after their months of working together she could see what he was thinking and she didn't like the picture.

"This side of the car or the other?" she asked. She cocked her pistol.

They didn't have very much time left. There was none remaining for introspection, hatred, regret or bitterness. There was only time enough to go down fighting.

With an effort that he hoped wasn't obvious to her, Lawson said, "Let's stay on the same side."

She nodded. "Good enough."

In silence, Junior's army charged the broken passenger car.

Ten.

THEY CAME FAST. SOME WERE faster than others. The most nimble hurtled through the windowframes and the gaping hole the horse-creatures had torn open. Lawson and Ann barely had an instant to take aim. Some moved like the wind, nearly invisible until they were right there, lower jaw unhinging, mouth straining wide, fangs sliding out for the feeding under the crimson glare of the eyes.

The first one Ann shot in the head wore the flesh of a little blond girl about ten years old, but there was caked blood all down the front of her lavender-colored dress and she shrieked like a storm of ravens as she burned. Lawson killed a young male vampire who had a deep jagged scar across his forehead, the testament of a hard human life. The fangs of a red-haired woman in the sackcloth dress of a farmer's wife came at Lawson before he shot her between the eyes and she fell back hissing like a snake and cracking like old plaster. Ann missed with her next shot at a gaunt male vampire in a filthy mud-colored suit, but Lawson got him in the left temple as he scrabbled toward Eli Easterly.

A female vampire with long dark hair and a nearly-skeletal body had leaped upon Gantt, who tried to fight her off but was no match for her strength. Lawson saw two vampires, a male and female, bearing Rooster down to the floorboards. Eric was firing his pistol, hitting nothing but at least keeping them back. Mathias was fighting a pair of vampires using the Winchester as a club. Lawson suddenly had the grinning rictus of an old white-haired man right in his face, and he shot the thing just below the left eye as it opened its mouth to bite. Ann killed another young female vampire, a golden-haired girl in a yellow dress who was still beautiful and who might have been in another life a stage actress or some celebrated but ultimately doomed soul.

Both Ann and Lawson were running out of bullets and had no time to reload. Then a blurred form fell upon him and a tremendous strength bore him down, and he looked up into the gap-toothed face of Henry Styles Junior, the one-hundred-and-five-year-old vampire boy.

Ann was pushed down by a wiry vampire with a thatch of black hair wild with cowlicks. Her gunhand was knocked aside just as her last silver bullet was fired.

"Ssssuch a sssstubborn fool," Junior said, as delicately as if already tasting him. His mouth opened and the fangs slid out. One hand was on Lawson's throat. A knee pinned the gunfighter's Colt. "We win, Trevor," he said in a whisper. "You ssssee? Firssst we win the battle, and then we win the—"

He blinked.

There had been a disturbance, a movement of something unseen, a something that should not be. Lawson felt it, just as Junior had.

Junior's head twisted around.

In the splintered mass of the car's side there appeared a figure, standing over Junior and Lawson.

It was an Indian with a single eagle feather in his braided hair. He was barechested but wore an open cowhide waistcoat decorated with patterns of red, blue and green beads. He held a sawed-off shotgun, the double barrels of which he pressed against Junior's forehead.

Lawson said to Junior, and afterward never knew why he spoke it: "Merry Christmas."

The Indian pulled both triggers.

There was no sacred work of the silver bullet in this. There was no butcher knife to cleave off the vampire boy's head. There was only a double load of buckshot, delivered at flesh-kissing range from a fearsome weapon held by a determined killer.

In the next instant Henry Styles Junior had no head. From the ragged mess of where it had been the black ichor streamed out, and the Indian grasped the neck of the writhing body and drank from it.

Lawson, in a kind of shocked stupor, realized he was seeing something he had never expected to witness: a vampire Indian, probably a Sioux by the look of him. He roused himself and used his last silver bullet to shoot in the midst of its cowlicks the creature who was bearing down on Ann. As that thing convulsed and burned, the Indian had already reloaded two shells and had strode forward to blow the head off one of the vampires who drank from Rooster. Then he grabbed by the hair a female who was gnawing into Deuce Mathias's back and he threw her through one of the windowframes as if she were made of straw. As the Indian was reloading for another vampire scalp, a second half-seen figure that had been moving with the quickness of the Dead Society slowed enough to come into view: a broad-shouldered, white-bearded mountain man in fringed buckskins and a coonskin cap. With a howl of rage he went to work with the axe he was carrying, causing heads with fanged mouths to fly and ichor to pour thickly from the neckstumps.

The appearance of a third figure, immediately following, was enough to send the remnants of Junior's army scrabbling from the car. This one was another male, slim of build, dressed in patched but relatively clean clothing and a dark blue jacket, and the axe he wielded did the same quick and violent work as the burly mountain man's. The bodies of the decapitated vampires continued to thrash, the arms flailing as if seeking the heads they'd lost, but the wound was too severe for the ichor or the lifeforce of the creatures to heal and their motions were slowing. A female vampire in blood-crusted rags showed either extreme hunger, courage or stupidity as she leaped upon the mountain man's back. Her fangs sank into his shoulder but her head was blown apart by the Indian's shotgun and all that was left were the curved teeth. The mountain man plucked them out with disdain and flung them away, then he grasped the twitching body to take his own drink.

They were on the run. A couple more dared to attack the new trio and were dispatched by the axes. After that, the passenger car emptied of the last of them. Lawson caught sight of the remaining troops, a paltry number, fleeing through the snow down the embankment into the woods. The winged shapechangers took to the air. A few half-hearted shots were fired from the rocks on the left, and then there was no more gunfire. The arms of Junior's headless body reached out as if trying to grasp hold of a purchase enough to stand. The hands with their dirty clawlike nails closed on empty air. Then the arms fell back, as from the stump of the neck the last of his ichor oozed out like ebony mud.

Lawson stood up. As he warily watched the new arrivals, he reloaded his Colt with silvers by holding the gun as best he could in his right hand; the broken arm was an impediment but at least he had a little strength in his fingers now. Ann was standing too, her face and hair splattered with vampire gore. Her expression was eerily calm, but her hands were shaking as she fed her pistol.

The Indian pushed two more shells in the shotgun. The mountain man swung his axe back and rested it on his shoulder. The vampire in the blue jacket leaned on his axe and looked around at the carnage.

"Travel this way often?" he asked. It was the voice of a refined and educated man.

"Once will be enough," Trevor said.

The man's eyes were light brown. There was a combination in them of both terrible sadness and terrible ferocity. Though his mouth was stained with the ichor his fangs had sucked from the bodies that still convulsed on the floorboards, he might have given the merest hint of a smile. It was hard to tell, because the light came only from flickering pools of lamp oil.

"You're one of us," he said.

"I'm one," Trevor answered. "Who are *us*?"

The man grunted softly. He was nearly Lawson's height, had thick black hair with streaks of gray on the sides and a gray lock that fell across his forehead above the right eye. On the left side of his face was the puckered round hole where a bullet had made its entry, and on the right side the same where it had made its exit. Another scar was scrawled from the corner of his left eye to the left corner of his mouth, and the disfigurement of the upper lip made him appear to wear the faint and rather mocking smile.

Minie ball hole and saber scar, Lawson thought. "The War For Southern Independence?" he asked.

"The War of the Rebellion," said the man.

"I was taken at Shiloh."

"You mean Pittsburg Landing? I was taken at Antietam."

"You mean, of course, Sharpsburg," said Lawson. "I was a captain."

"I was a major…captain."

"Ah," Lawson said, and returned the smile in same faint and mocking fashion. "Well…we are greatly thankful for your arrival here, major. *All* of us."

"Figure you'd best see to your people," rumbled the mountain man. "Smellin' their blood."

Except for Ann, the others had become a frozen tableau…and almost literally because the air was far below freezing, the snowfall heavier, and the car looked to have been busted and crushed by the fist and boot of a disagreeable giant who hated trains. It was time to count the costs.

Blue was all right, drifting in and out with no knowledge of any of this. Easterly had taken some splinters and glass cuts, but he'd had the presence of mind in the battle to draw his crucifix and use it to burn the creatures who'd tried to swarm both himself and the girl. Eric had suffered the rake of a claw from the top of his left shoulder down to the elbow and been bitten on the throat but the vampire's thirst had been interrupted by the noise of the Indian's shotgun. With the decapitation of Junior the creature had decided a few cupfuls of human blood was enough soup for the nightly meal and had fled the car through a window.

Mathias had fought them off as well, though he'd taken several bites to both arms, his hands and one more frenzied bite on his back. He was weak and dazed but he was alive.

"I'M ALL RIGHT," said Rooster as he struggled to his feet. What had saved him was the fact that the male and female vampires who'd attacked him had started fighting each other for his blood. The female had gotten to his neck while the male's fangs had pierced his right hand, but just after the male had been destroyed by the shotgun the female had pulled out and turned away in time to give her head to an axeblade. "I'm all right," Rooster repeated, though he had lost a goodly amount of blood and was near falling down again. "I'm ready for the nuthouse, but I'm all right."

"Gantt?" Lawson called. There was no answer.

The mountain man had already walked back to the strongest smell of human blood.

"This one's gone," he said. "Throat open…chest too. Heart's tore out." He glanced at Lawson with a pair of narrow pale blue eyes in the rugged and wrinkled face. "Took it and skedaddled. Blood trail goes out the window."

Lawson had to see for himself. He hated the sight, for Gantt's eyes were open and blood had run from both corners of his mouth. It seemed a terrible violation, worse than having your throat pierced by a pair of fangs, to have your heart torn out and stolen as one might snatch a gravy-soaked biscuit from a dinner plate. He recalled seeing a very thin female vampire with long dark hair bearing down on Gantt. He wondered if it might have been Eva, and if so…LaRouge was teaching her well.

He had no doubt LaRouge was somewhere near. Maybe not in the Montana territory, but near enough to have planned all this, and near enough to soon know that Lawson had escaped.

But he and the other survivors had not gotten out of it yet. Helena still seemed a world away…and there were these three to be considered.

"Josephus Wilder," said the mountain man. "Your handle?"

"Trevor Lawson. Your name?" he asked the major.

The man was standing over Reverend Easterly and Blue, and the Indian was walking back and forth among the dying vampire bodies.

"Achilles Godfrey," said the man.

That name. That name, Lawson thought. Where had he—?

Oh yes.

"Major Godfrey," said Lawson. "Also known as 'Godless'."

"By some," the major said. "Those who failed to grasp realities."

"I read in the newspaper…somewhere…about you and your men at the battle of Boonsboro."

"You mean the battle of South Mountain."

"The Yankee name for it. Specifically, what happened at Fox's Gap. September 14th, 1862…three days before Sharpsburg. Does that bring back a memory?"

"Dim," came the answer. "All of that, except for that night on the Antietam battlefield, among the screaming wounded, when *they* found me under my dead horse… very dim."

"I'll refresh your memory. Sixty Confederate bodies thrown down a well in the aftermath of Fox's Gap. Thrown down there like garbage. Did you piss on them afterward?"

"Trevor," said Ann. "*Don't.*"

Lawson realized that the vampire Indian had moved slightly to one side and nearer him, the better to get a clear line-of-fire with the loaded shotgun.

"I call him Smoke, because he moves so quickly and quietly," said Achilles Godfrey, in a soft and beguiling voice. "He doesn't speak. I saved his life many years ago from a pack of *them*. His own kind, turned. He has repeated the favor many times. We are all brothers here, and there are several more out there who came with us to dispatch as many as possible. We have a small community a few miles away, in the mountains. We felt them gathering. We sent out scouts. Smoke is not the only Sioux in our happy little town. Imagine our amazement...that instead of humans being trapped as food for *them*, aboard this train is one of *us*. We saw you talking to that...boy, and what happened afterward. It was quite a shock to me personally, but then again...there had to be others like us out there. *Had* to be."

"Like you? How?"

Godfrey was slow in answering. He walked over to a puddle of burning oil and stared into it, and by that light Lawson caught the red glare in the eyes of his battle-scarred face. "Ex-Captain Lawson," he said, "that war you refer to with understandable bitterness is over. Yet there is another war that has been going on for years... centuries...that shows no signs of abatement. You are either on one side or another, and I will term those the dark and the light. May I call you Trevor?"

Lawson nodded. He realized he owed his continuation of existence and the life of the others to this man, to Wilder and to Smoke, but...*Achilles Godfrey*? One of the most malicious and hate-filled officers to ever wear the Union blue? The story of the sixty bodies and the well had been verified, but what of the other tales? The quick execution of prisoners both by firing squad and hanging? The burning-to-the-ground of Southern villages removed from any military purpose? The placement of severed heads atop fenceposts as markers to show where the troops of Major Godless had passed through? And the skinning of the two camp followers who were proven to be Confederate spies...

All those things Lawson had read about in newspapers in the aftermath of the conflict, as more witnesses had come forward and facts revealed. But who knew where Major Godless had disappeared to? He was one of the many hundreds missing from the battlefield, yet his legacy was still a matter of heated discussion in the papers of the day. Lawson recalled sitting in the lobby of the Hotel Sanctuaire not a year ago and reading that a new common grave of Confederate dead had been found on farmland west of Fox's Gap. Of the thirty or so soldiers most were headless, yet it appeared a few had been buried alive with their arms severed at the shoulders. This was reported to be the work of Achilles Godfrey and his troops from a drummer boy who had escaped the carnage.

"Trevor," said the major, "this war is one we cannot lose. We have decided to fight the inhumanity that is attempting to consume us. We drink animal blood, not human…except for the occasional freshly-dead body we must dig up from graveyards. We portion that out in shares. The body is returned to the coffin and the earth, and no one is the wiser. We can hold out for a few months between feedings. As I say, we subsist mostly on animal blood." His gaze sharpened as he looked upon Lawson. "I suspect your so-called life is the same?"

"I haven't sunken to grave-robbing."

"You mean…you haven't sunken to grave-robbing *yet*."

"You've started drinking the ichor? That sustains you?" Lawson recalled his own brief and bitter taste of LaRouge's ichor at the mansion in Nocturne.

"We have been victorious in a few small skirmishes and have learned to drink from our enemies when possible," Godfrey said. "It's a particularly vile liquid but we've found that it *does* give strength…though not anything like the power of human blood. You've never tasted it?"

"Only once."

"Listen…please…maybe I shouldn't oughta be hearin' this?" Rooster asked.

"I don't think I ought to be, either," Mathias added. "It doesn't sound too healthy for a regular man to know."

"We need to get this girl to the hospital in Helena," Lawson told the major. "Rooster, can you drive this train?"

"I can drive, but can you shovel coal?"

"I can try," said Eric. He had wrapped cloth torn from his coat around his wounded shoulder. "I'm not hurt bad enough to want to just sit here and *wait*."

"The track's still blocked," Mathias said. "What about that?"

"It's nothing we can't move," the major answered. "As I say, we've brought others. They're standing guard around the train...what's left of it." He looked back and forth along the car. "I expect we should remove these bodies before you get to Helena. There's going to be enough to have to explain to the sheriff and the railroad company as it is."

"Holy Lord!" said Rooster, with renewed alarm. "And me the only one left of the crew! They'll split me in four pieces and hang every one of 'em!"

"We'll figure something out," Lawson said. "Ann and I will stay in Helena as witnesses to a bandit raid."

"What...*bitin'* bandits? They'll laugh me right into the prison hole!"

"I'll have a talk with the sheriff. I can be very convincing when it's necessary." One benefit of his condition was that the Eye could be used to sap a victim's strength of will and turn his or her mind into clay that could be shaped to suit the purpose. Even so, it seemed he and Ann would have a lot of claywork to do in Helena.

"I'll verify whatever Lawson says," said Easterly. "We are not going to let anyone suffer any further."

"We?" Lawson lifted his eyebrows. "*We?*"

Easterly came toward him and stopped only a couple of feet away. He cast his gaze upon Wilder, Smoke and Godfrey before it came back to Lawson.

"I am everything you already know," he said. "I have lived in the blackest of shadows. I have done terrible things, in my own name and in the name of God. I have lost...the most precious gift that was given to me: my family." He lowered his head, and it was a moment before he could speak again. "I have nothing now," he said, his voice strained by emotion. "I have been a thief, a charlatan, a wife-beater, a drunk, a joke of a father, a false prophet, and a back-shooting bounty hunter.

"But, Mr. Lawson," he said, and he lifted his eyes to the vampire's, "I have never been a *soldier.* Would you allow me that honor?"

"A dubious honor," Lawson replied. "One that may kill you...or present you with something worse than death."

"I am already beyond that point," said the reverend. "I am dead now...and I would like to return to something that might be called *life.*"

Easterly meant it. Lawson didn't have to throw his Eye to see that.

"We'll talk in Helena," he said.

"Shall we start removing this trash?" Godfrey asked. "Then we'll get to work on the rocks."

Lawson was still in no shape to be moving bodies, as his broken right arm had not yet mended. He sat down on a bullet-nicked seat as Godfrey, Smoke, Wilder, and Easterly began to haul the dead vampires out of the car and throw them into the woods below. Ann sat on a seat facing him. Tears had rolled down her cheeks, but her expression was still eerily composed. She had to break sometime, Lawson thought. It might be tomorrow or the next few days, but sooner or later she would break.

Then he would help Ann put herself back together again, and they would go on.

"Trevor?" Her voice seemed distant. "*Trevor?*" she repeated.

"Yes?"

"Did I kill my father?"

He looked her square in the eyes, trying to give her as much of his strength that he could spare. "You know the answer to that."

She nodded, but even as she did two fresh tears spilled.

He reached out with his good arm and took her hand. There was nothing more he could say, and nothing more she could ask. She shivered from the cold, and the snow blew into her hair and the puddles of lamp fuel flickered, and the bodies of the vampires were thrown into the woods and at one point Ann removed the pistol from her holster, put it on the seat beside her and stared at it as if it were the most hateful enemy she had ever faced. Then after awhile she put it back into its holster, where it belonged.

When the bodies were cleared out, the vampires along with Eli Easterly began the removal of the rocks. Eric and Rooster went out to watch, and Rooster wanted to go over the process of bringing the locomotive up to steam. Ann informed Lawson that Blue was waking up, and he went back to kneel beside her.

She was still very pale and obviously in great need of the surgery, but her voice was stronger when she spoke. Her eyes, at first unfocused, found Lawson. "Am I… guh…guh…gonna die?"

"No. We'll be getting you to the hospital in Helena very soon. Just hang on a little longer."

She gave a small laugh that must have hurt, because she winced. Then she said, "If there's…anything Ca… Ca…Cassie Fredricks can d…do…it's h…h…hang on."

"Cassie," Lawson said quietly, and he put a hand on her forehead. "That's my daughter's name."

With an effort, she moved her head away. "Ohhhh," she whispered, "your h…hand's so c…*cold*."

"I'm sorry," he told her. He had forgotten for a moment what he was. He waited until she slept again, and then he stood up. He saw Deuce Mathias sitting on the remnant of a seat toward the front, bent over with his hands to his face, and he crunched across the debris of timbers and glass to the man, who looked up when he heard someone coming.

Lawson leaned down close, and he saw Mathias's face tighten with fear.

"When we reach Helena," Lawson said, "you are going to start walking. Go in any direction you please, but never look back." He held up a finger when Mathias started to speak. "Don't question. Consider your life from this point on to be a second chance. I think you've earned it. *Shut,*" he said when again Mathias opened his mouth, and then Lawson turned away before good sense and a reward for a common killer changed his mind.

It didn't take much longer before Achilles Godfrey and Easterly returned to the car. Steam had begun to billow along the tracks. Some of it would be coming into the car, along with the wind and the snow and coalsparks, but Lawson doubted that anyone would complain too much about their open-air condition as long as the car held together. Easterly went back to again stand watch over Cassie Fredricks. Ann sat alone with her thoughts. Deuce Mathias sat alone with a new future ahead of him and a past night that he knew no one on earth would believe. The bodies of Keene Presco, Johnny Rebinaux, Glorious George Gantt and the skin of Jack Tabberson had joined the dead vampires in the wooded embankment below the tracks, and this was an area where the predators were always hungry.

"I have questions," Godfrey said to Lawson. "Do you have any idea why this filth gathered in such numbers here, and why they went to such effort? I doubt they were after only the humans."

"They want me, and my friend Ann."

"Decidedly so. And why might that be? Do you pose a particular threat to them?"

"Resistance is a threat," said Lawson.

"Yes, but…is there anything more I should know? Evidently they hold you and your friend in dangerous regard. The bullets you were using…what of those?"

"Silver bullets blessed with holy water by a priest."

"Ah. So you've discovered a better way to kill them than with shotgun blast and axeblade?"

Lawson was a little late in answering, so the major went on. "I believe we should meet again. In fact, I insist upon it. I'd like to hear your story. Where might I find you?"

Lawson retrieved his wallet and gave him one of the plain white cards. Beneath Lawson's name and the address of the Hotel Sanctuaire was the line *All Matters Handled*. And below that…

"I travel by night," Godfrey read. "Were you trying to be humorous?"

"No. Realistic."

"Well...New Orleans is a distance and I too would be forced to travel by night. But I think it would be a journey worth taking. There are not many of us who fight against this, Trevor. We need to form our own army, and we need a plan of battle."

"Agreed."

"I'll visit you there. When, I'm not sure. But soon." Godfrey put the card away in a pocket of his jacket. Was he smiling, or was this just the wound of his face? "I do recall Antietam," he said. "The night I was taken. And the one who turned me. Oh yes, I do remember her."

"Her?"

"A woman who calls herself LaRouge. A very beautiful monster, Trevor. This is who I search for, and you can believe I'll never give up. Do you know the myth?"

Lawson was unable to speak.

"The myth...that consuming the ichor of the one who has turned you will turn you *back* to being fully human again? Is it a myth, or is it truth? I don't know, but I do know that I want to die as a human, and nothing on God's Heaven or in Satan's Hell will stop me from finding that monster and draining every drop of ichor from her body. She is *mine* to kill." Godfrey put a hand on Lawson's shoulder. "That keeps me going, Trevor. It keeps me wanting to live. But as you must know, I was always inflamed by the idea of revenge."

"Yes," said Lawson, and it was the only word he could think to say.

"I will see you in New Orleans. You may count on that. And then I shall be ready to lead our army into a war we *must* win." Did the eyes spark, or was it a shine of madness?

"Goodbye for now, Captain," said Major Godless, who gave the soldier from Alabama a brief salute before he went out the door beyond which the silent Smoke was waiting. They drifted off together, along with the other figures that moved through the snow.

The train gave a lurch. The iron wheels turned. The damaged car squealed and cried out, but it held together as the locomotive rolled onward through where a pile of boulders had been, with a little boy perched on the biggest one.

Lawson had to sit down, before he fell.

The last train from Perdition was going home.